B&T 8.74

ASK ME NO QUESTIONS

By Ann Schlee

NOVEL
Rhine Journey

FOR YOUNG READERS
The Vandal
The Guns of Darkness
The Consul's Daughter
The Strangers

Ask Me No Questions

Ann Schlee

Holt, Rinehart and Winston
New York

Library of Congress Cataloging in Publication Data
Schlee, Ann.
Ask me no questions.
Summary: Laura, sent to the country from London to
escape the cholera in 1848, tries to help the neglected
children of Drouet's asylum she finds eating the pigs'
food in her uncle's barn.
[1. Child abuse—Fiction. 2. Poverty—Fiction.
3. Orphans—Fiction. 4. England—Fiction] I. Title.
PZ7.S3468As 1982   [Fic]   81-6932   AACR2

ISBN 0-03-061523-2

First American Edition

Printed in the United States of America
1 3 5 7 9 10 8 6 4 2

To my grandmother

CHAPTER ONE

The cow began to bellow early in the morning and the sound roused Laura. She woke in the little attic room where they had put her the night before, knowing herself to be in a strange place but for a few seconds holding from her the awareness of where she was. It seemed by doing so that she was in no place and might almost wake where she chose.

But do what she would, images of her arrival appeared behind her tightly closed eyes. She was high up in a house. Her aunt's black skirts had dragged up the stairs in front of her for at least two flights. The candle had radiated against dark spaces Laura had no knowledge of. It sent shadows of the banisters gliding silently down the wall as they climbed upwards, as if a procession of ghosts were vacating the rooms they were about to enter. She did not like this place. She had not wanted to come, but there had been no choice. The cholera had come to their father's parish and she and her younger brother, Barty, must come away the seven miles from London to the countryside where it was safe.

Papa could not come away. He must continue to go into the cottages where he would not let her or Barty go. As a minister of God he must fight all his life against that great injustice that caused the poor people to die before they understood that God loved them too and wanted them to be good. If they were going to die of cholera he must work the harder to explain to them before it was too late. It was a great opportunity. And as he must not desert his parishioners, so Mama must not desert him. All this Laura understood, and that she must be in this house with these people, but it could not make her want to be here.

For a long time, it seemed, before they climbed the stairs, they had been kept standing in a lamplit parlour crowded with dark imposing furniture. There her Uncle Bolinger, grocer and vestryman, had tucked his thumbs into the little pockets at either end of his watch-chain and said, "Your cholera's a rum animal. There's not everyone that understands it."

Does he? Laura had thought. I doubt he does. His face had been moist when he kissed her and he breathed the rich warm fearful smell that comes through the swing doors of beer shops.

Through the doors of the beer shop near her home she had heard the poor people singing:

The cholera's coming, oh dear, oh dear,
The cholera's coming, oh dear!

Their voices were jolly as if they were teasing, but the words were sad because it *had* come. In the paper on Papa's desk in his study there was a picture. Cholera was a skeleton in a black cloak and rowed on the water. Its hands on the oars were bones. You could see its bony knees, its ribs; its face was a skull. The people that worked in the sandpits at the edge of the parish had the cholera. Every day they died. Maybe the very ones that sang in the beer shop had died.

Before Uncle Bolinger could say what it was that he knew and no one else understood, a little old maid-servant had run forward and hugged and kissed her right across her face, and wept that Miss Lottie's child had grown taller than she in all the years that had passed. That was Amy her mother had told her about. There was to be another person too, her Cousin Henry, who they had told her several times would come tomorrow from Oxford where he was studying to enter the church as her papa had done.

All these people waited now somewhere outside this room, all to be faced again. If only by willing it so, she might open her eyes to find a fraction of the flowered wallpaper of her room at home! She kept her eyes shut a moment longer, and lying like that heard for the first time distinctly the shuddering cry of the cow.

Laura sat up and opened her eyes. At the foot of the bed was a narrow dormer window hung over with a brown patch of curtain. She ran over the bare boards with her bare feet, pushed aside the curtain, rubbed on the cold clouded glass with her fist and looked down. There was a muddy road and houses — no people, no cow.

She did not know whether her uncle owned a cow. Indeed it might belong to anyone in the village, but clearly it was in trouble. She imagined it fallen in a ditch or trapped in a hedge, and in need of help, appealing directly to her. Its cries were pitiable.

While she pulled on her heavy winter clothes she heard again the high straining sound as if it were being torn in two. Someone must hear it, she thought, someone will go to it. She dared not leave the room without all her clothes and with her hair not dressed, for in the passage might be her aunt.

In the dark wooden frame of the little mirror her own fingers worked busily down one long plait of hair and then down the other. Her same face stayed quite still, one cheek blotched by the stain that spread up from the corner of the old glass so that involuntarily she rubbed her cheek with her hand before she thought to move her head.

Coming here in the cart at night, holding tightly to Barty's hand, she had stared out the window. Outside in the dark but keeping pace as the moon does on winter walks was the dim reflection of her own face. It seemed more truly her than the person who solidly occupied her seat within the cart: a new child come to haunt the old familiar one. She had not been able to take her eyes from it.

When her ribbons were tied she ran into the room across the landing where Barty had slept. He was awake, sitting up in bed with the covers pulled around him, sucking in long shivering breaths between his rattling teeth but making no move to get up and dressed. "Get up," she said. "Can't you hear the cow?"

She could hear him clicking together under the blankets the two little oxtail bones that cook had given him. He kept them in his pockets and played with them when he was not happy.

Barty lifted his dark hair off his face and said, "What's the matter with it?"

"Well I don't know," said Laura crossly. "Get dressed. You're cold." She wondered if he had cried last night.

"Go away," he said. "I'm not getting dressed with you in here."

Laura went out again onto the landing. The window in Barty's room had been let into the same wall as her own, so it too would face the front. Now she saw another door next to her own. It might lead to a servant's bedroom but no servant would be still abed. She tapped gently at the door. No answer. She looked about her and slowly turned the knob, peering quickly through the crack. A rich winey smell and a pleasing smell of dust filled her nose and throat. She went inside and shut the door quickly behind her so that none of it would escape. On one side of the little room, dust sheets lay over strange angular shapes. On the other, pale puckered apples were spread in neat rows on the floor and there, just where she had hoped, was a bare window looking to the back of the house, its corners rounded off with cobwebs.

Laura undid the catch and pushing open the casement, leaned out. Below was a paved yard, then a gate, then a rough orchard of apple trees with a few blackened leaves and wizened fruit abandoned in their upper branches. Beyond she saw a cluster of black clapboard barns. That was where the cow must be.

11

Laura felt excited. No one had told her that this was a farm. Behind the barn she could see the dark winter fields crossed now by muddy hedges, now by a wide shining ditch, until they came to a row of black trees drawn flat against the sky like skeletal leaves. Nothing moved except a cluster of rooks tossed and left to fall in the cold currents of air.

To the right of her aunt's house she could see an inn yard cluttered with straw and barrels. It had rained in the night and each barrel held a disc of dully-shining water. To the left stretched a long bare yard running along the far side of her aunt's orchard wall, the earth all trampled bare and pitted like a road. Here and there on its surface a sullen puddle had gathered.

Laura had thought at first that this place was quite deserted. Now she heard a sound, *slap, slap, slap*, repeated steadily somewhere on the ground. Something moved. She leant further over the sill. There between the wall and the next door house, in the near corner of the great deserted yard, a solitary child was skipping with a rope. Determinedly the rope hit the ground: *four ... five ... six ....* It was a girl. Laura saw her plait bounce on her neck, but how big was she? Only her head and arms showed. The rope arched steadily above them. *Seven ... eight ... nine ....* How warm she must keep, thought Laura, for the swinging arms rose bare from the girl's pinafore and Laura standing with the same cold air blowing in on her shivered in all her winter clothes. Still she continued to hang from the window and count. *Ten ... eleven ... twelve ....* She herself had once reached eighty-four without stumbling.

But as she watched, as the possibility of a friendship formed in her mind, she noticed that the pinafore was ragged and dirty. She is a poor person's child, thought Laura sadly. She stopped counting and a moment later she shut the window and went to look for Barty.

He was ready, and together they went down the stairs looking curiously about them at the house where they might be staying for a whole month. It looked smaller and less imposing than it had the night before by candlelight. The stairs to the attics were bare, but on the next landing and the next flight there was matting, and then on the stairs visible from the entrance there was dark brown carpet. At the divide between the matting and the carpet they stood and watched the maidservant on the floor below carry a tray out of a room to the left of the front door. That was where breakfast would be. When she had disappeared into the kitchen they went quietly down and pushed open the door of the room. Their Aunt and Uncle Bolinger sat facing each other on either end of a table drawn up before the parlour fire.

Their aunt set down her cup with a little click and said, "Is this the time your mother lets you come to breakfast? What can she be thinking of?"

"I beg your pardon," said Laura politely, "but no one called us."

"Hoity toity," said her aunt with a sidelong look at her husband. "If you think Amy has nothing better to do at this hour than to climb all those stairs after you, you'd best think again."

It was not kind to say that, yet nor did she say it in anger. Am I meant to kiss her? thought Laura. Aunt

Bolinger did not hold out her arms or make any move towards her but sitting quite still, with a peremptory move of her head she offered her heavy cheek. Laura leant forward and touched it with her cheek. Her aunt smelt of soap and lavender water. Laura sensed that the kiss had pleased her. Some people when they smile loosen their mouths, but Aunt Bolinger's, though it curved, became more compressed. It had a commanding quality. "Sit down," she said.

Barty was spared the ceremony of the kiss. He sat and stared at this woman who should have been like his mother and was not and so was doubly unfamiliar. Her bosom rose hard and black and shining above the white cloth. It seemed to him that she was not made of flesh at all but of solid rolls and pads of that same black shiny material that made up her dress.

Laura broke her bread and sipped her hot milk before she found courage to say, "Uncle Bolinger, have you a cow? Because I heard a cow crying."

Uncle Bolinger cleared his throat and dabbed at his lips and eyes with his table napkin. He looked at his wife and then at his plate and said, "Yes. It's Bessy and don't you fret about it. She'll do."

"Is she in pain?" persisted Laura.

"No, she is not," said her aunt decidedly.

"She'll be happy enough by nightfall," said Uncle Bolinger. Neither of them said anything more, but Laura sensed the repression of some truth. All she could do was to listen and hope it might reveal itself.

"Let's have a look at you by daylight then," said Aunt Bolinger and they both turned to Laura, searching with brief interest not for her but for her mother's vanished girlhood or whatever in her was family and common to them. Barty, who was very like his father, they ignored.

"You've your mother's fine eyes, my dear," said Uncle Bolinger and began at once upon a fit of coughing which he buried in his napkin.

"There was never anything special about Lottie's eyes that I noticed," said Aunt Bolinger. "And she's her father's complexion, poor child. But she's a Dunning in feature. She's a look of my mother's sister Fanny, has she not, Mr Bolinger?"

"What are we to do today?" asked Barty.

"Do what you please," said Aunt Bolinger smartly. "But you are to keep out of my house till dinner time. Laura may help in the kitchen, but you're to keep outside, and you're not to play and cause a commotion near the house."

"I'll be away to the barn," said Uncle Bolinger, getting heavily to his feet and winking inexplicably at Laura, "to see how the old cow is."

"You'll do no such thing, when you've kept us all awake coughing half the night! We've a cowman to see to the cow."

Laura felt sorry for him. He looked so disappointed. He had really wanted to go. She helped to carry the breakfast things into the kitchen and when she next looked round for Barty he had gone.

When Laura had dried the knives and forks, Amy asked her to feed the hens. She was standing in the same

15

yard she had seen from the upstairs storeroom, scattering grain, when she saw Barty come running towards her through the trees of the orchard. "Come quickly," he said. "The calf's being born. If you're quick you can see."

"Is that what's the matter with it?"

"Yes," he said scornfully as if he had known all along.

"*She* didn't want us to know about it," said Laura, looking back apprehensively towards the house, but her curiosity was enormous. No fear could check it. She began to run after Barty, compelled to know what he meant. For things were "not-yet-born," although people always seemed to know that they would be, and then quite suddenly they were born. They were there as babies. Barty had been there, quite complete, one morning in a cot by a window in her mother's room, in the house they had lived in when Laura was a little girl, with a tiny fist set with real fingernails pressed against his mouth. But "being born" as an act that took up time in itself—that went on happening in all the time it took Barty to run from the barn to the house and back again—that was an entirely new idea.

The path between the apple trees widened out into an unfenced yard scattered with straw and pitted with hoof marks and wheel ruts in which the slurry of the animals had collected, green and shining. To one side two great frowning pigs worked their way over the bare earth of a small copse. No blade of grass, no shoot of green was left. Their strong snouts had rubbed it quite bare, but still they browsed absorbedly as if out of habit. They

16

paid no attention to Laura for which she was grateful. She kept her distance, crossing the yard as close to the barn wall as she could. The high barn door was open. Barty waited, beckoning importantly, until she had nearly caught up with him. Then he slipped through it and disappeared. She heard a man's voice say in a strong pleased tone, "It's come just now. It's a little one. Just slid right out."

Out of what? thought Laura. It just slid out of what? She was inside the barn. How strange it was and large, filled with twilight air that smelt richly of hay and dung. The indistinct walls, the great high roof were patched with grey outdoor light where tiles and boards had broken or rotted away. Where the light from the doorway penetrated the gloom of the barn, Laura saw a man, he would be the cowman. He looked up and said sharply to her, "Does your aunt know you're here, miss?"

"Barty's here," said Laura.

"She might not want you here at this time," said the man slowly.

"Why can he be here and I can't?" insisted Laura. She was panting from running and felt wronged and oddly close to tears.

"I don't want to get across her," said the man doubtfully.

"We won't tell. I promise." She was looking about her all the time and now she thought crossly: Why does it matter anyway? For whatever the secret enactment had been, she had come too late.

The cow lay slumped on the straw. There was a patch

17

of blood on her white knee. A few paces from her there lay the dark shape of the calf. It was all wet, like something dragged from the river. Its head was very large; its eyes hooded and swollen like an enormous insect's. It repelled her. It was not an animal at all but still part of some unearthly life. Where has it come from? Where has it come from? The question was insistent. She would not move until she knew.

"Is it alive?" whispered Barty. He went forward and squatted down in the straw staring at it. Laura stayed where she was.

"It's all right for now," said the cowman. Then with a change of voice he spoke to the calf. "Here, better bring you over. She'll never find you down there." He stood up and going to the calf took one of its long forelegs in each hand and dragged it over the straw to the cow. It seemed wrong to Laura that he was not at all gentle with it. Then she saw with a start that his arms were glistening with pale bright blood.

"Why is there blood on your arms?"

"There's always a bit of blood at a birth." He knelt down and taking up a handful of straw began to clean himself.

"Are you hurt?" asked Laura quickly. Instinctively she knew it was not his blood, but she could think of no other way to ask.

"Bless you no," he said with a laugh. "It's the old cow's blood."

"Is *she* hurt?" There was no need to ask. She had known quite well that the cow cried out of pain. The aunt had told her an untruth.

"Not now. She bellowed a bit but she's happy enough now."

That was true. The cow dragged her tongue contentedly over the ruckled fur of the little calf. The blood was not frightening. No one was harmed by it. There was a great peace in the barn. They were silent all three, listening to the rasping of the cow's tongue, aware of their own and each other's happiness.

"I doubt it'll live though," said the man. He gathered up an armful of straw and began to scatter it behind the cow.

"What do you mean?" cried Laura shocked. "Why should it die?"

"Why, it swallowed too much water inside its ma." How carelessly he spoke, continuing to scatter straw. Yet another part of her mind grabbed and repeated those words, *Inside its ma, inside its ma.* "Once they're born you hold them up and it all trickles out, but once they start to breathe they sucks it in again. It may have drowned itself by morning."

To lie drowning on the floor of the barn all surrounded by the dusty air. "Oh, it mustn't," cried Laura. At the same time that other region of her mind said in triumph, *It came from inside her. I knew it did.*

"Oh, I'm not bothered. It's a bull in any case. It's not worth much dead or alive. It might live. You can't keep them all."

To Laura it mattered more than anything in the world that it should live. She seemed to summon up all the strength in her own body and heap it on to the body in the straw. She had not liked it at all to begin with. Now

19

that it seemed it might die she planned to come each day and feed it and befriend it. It would love her. In a way it would be hers. She thought: If I want it to live I can make it live.

Now the cowman was heaping up straw around the cow to keep it warm. He said, "You'd best go now and I'd take it kindly if you said nothing to your aunt."

"We shan't tell," said Barty. Laura knew he would not; secrecy was habitual to him. She herself felt oddly untroubled at the prospect of having perhaps to tell a lie. She had only to keep secret her knowledge of what they would have cheated her of knowing. There was a simple enough way of doing so. As she ran back through the orchard she allowed to occur in her mind a complete divorce between what happened in the house and what happened in the barn.

CHAPTER TWO

That afternoon Laura was set to whip the seams of a pillow slip. She was told to sit in the windowseat in the drawing room where the light would serve her longest. Barty was set to read a book at a table near her. By twisting her head Laura could see that Barty's book was called *Missionary Strivings*. She wondered what it might be about. Some books with names like that were very exciting, and sometimes they were very dull, but you never knew until you had agreed to read them which they might be. Barty's eyes were fixed steadily on the page. His face was quite blank. He always looked like that when he read. Sometimes he read for hours at a time, but today she had only completed the first long seam when looking up she saw that he had fallen asleep, the book pushed to one side on the brown plush cloth, his thick black hair falling over his jacket sleeve.

Aunt Bolinger made no attempt to talk. She sat knitting sternly by the fire. When Uncle Bolinger reached down his long pipe from the chimney piece she said, "You know you're not to smoke that with Henry so soon to be in the house. Smoke it in the kitchen if you must, but not in here where it will upset him. You know he cannot abide the smell of it."

"He is not here yet," said Uncle Bolinger mildly.

"He will be soon enough. He'll notice it directly for it clings in the curtains."

Uncle Bolinger sighed and replaced his pipe and took his seat opposite to her.

As no one spoke to her, Laura of course did not have any obligation to speak herself. It rested her that she need not and that Barty was safely asleep. Besides she wanted to please her aunt by sewing neatly and to finish the task by daylight. After a while her aunt looked across to her. "Show me your work, Laura." Laura silently handed it over for inspection. "That is very neatly done," said Aunt Bolinger releasing her quick peremptory smile. "Do you like to sew?"

"I like to very much."

There was a dry laugh then. "Your mother always fancied herself at sewing." Yet surely on the whole she had been kind, and Laura felt pleased as she took her work back to the window.

When Barty woke and looked strangely about him, Aunt Bolinger said, "Would you both like to play outside before supper?" He was on his feet immediately, still dazed with sleep, making for the door.

"I have not quite finished yet," said Laura anxiously.

"Well, well," said her aunt, "it will keep till tomorrow. Be off with you. But don't be late for your dinner. Your cousin will not want to be kept waiting."

Outside in the passage Laura hesitated. She could

hear Barty's footsteps sounding up the stairs as he ran for his cap and muffler. She too had thought all afternoon, as she sewed, about the little calf, and longed just to go and reassure herself that it still lived. Yet now that she was free she felt a reluctance to go. The afternoon light lingered drably on the dark walls. The lamps were still unlit.

This was a time that she loved at home, when the approaching dark faltered: a time to draw curtains on the altering world outside before it altogether lost its rightful shapes, a time for gathering in, not venturing out.

That morning she had run with such anticipation through the orchard that she had scarcely looked about her. Now she remembered the bleak prospect from the storeroom window: the desolate yard, the lonely poor child next door, the neglected orchard, the drifting rooks. It would be dark in the barn. The calf might be there, dead. A sensation of emptiness grew and grew inside her and seemed to meet no boundary to contain it.

Barty would have no doubts about going. At any moment he would appear wrapped for the cold and be angry with her for delaying him. He would make her go, or worse, he would leave her behind. She began to run up the stairs and met him running down. "Hurry up," he said. "You're so slow."

Laura seized her cloak from its peg in her room and ran down again. In the kitchen, while Barty waited impatiently, she strapped on her pattens. Then he ran ahead of her across the yard into the orchard. "Wait,

wait," Laura called after him, bunching up her skirts and struggling to run in the clumsy pattens. There was light enough to see by, to kick away the rotting apples and avoid the roots, but the air held that waiting winter quality that will surrender quickly enough to the dark. Laura heard the noise of the rooks and looking up saw them floating lost in the wind. There were no stars. Against the sky the tangled branches were very black and the bright shrunken fruit that still hung out of reach looked unnatural to the trees. Their mossy trunks shone a strange unearthly green. She began to feel the cold in earnest.

Barty stopped before he came to the farmyard. Laura saw him scoop up an apple and hide it in his pocket. He must be made to throw it away before they went inside the house again. They ran on. The barn rose above them, still and large and black. Laura wondered if the savage pigs were free in their wood or if they had been shut inside. Better to think of the warm little calf lying beside his mother. But what if it were dead? It would not be warm then. She looked back towards the house and saw through the trees the faint squares of lamplight. That would be the kitchen, that the drawing room. They would just look at the calf. Then they would run back to the house.

She saw Barty lean against the door and wedge himself through the gap and thought again how dark the barn would be, but when she reached the door herself and felt the sweet breath of the barn on her face, she stopped feeling frightened and felt instead almost impelled to go on. The thick dark spaces opened out around her. She stood quite still until her eyes saw better. The chinks of light in the roof and walls seemed brighter than they had in the daytime. Some distance from the door the white patches on the cow's flank gleamed. She was standing, moving about over the straw. The calf would be somewhere near her.

"Can you see it?" she whispered to Barty. "Is it alive?" She hadn't the courage to go closer. Barty too stood where he was without moving forward, staring intently at the cow. "I think she's licking it," he whispered. "She wouldn't bother if it were dead." It was true they could hear the rasping sound of her tongue.

It was a great relief to Laura. She took Barty by the hand and would have ventured closer to the cow, but at that moment there was a sound of footsteps squelching in the mud outside and broken snatches of whistling. Barty's hand tightened on hers. He began to pull her away from the door to where a high untidy stack of hay leant against a wooden partition. Without a word he began to scramble up it. "I can't go up there," whispered Laura after him. "I'll get all covered." But all the same she too began to climb the unsteady stack, slipping and half choking in the thick sweet dust raised by Barty's boots. Near the top was a level space. Here Barty stretched himself and stared over the edge. Laura lay beside him and watched the tall door slowly open.

The cowman must have heard a sound, for he held up the lantern and circled it slowly in front of him, squinting into the dark spaces beyond the area of grey light by the door. He hung the lantern on a post and went outside again. "He heard us," whispered Barty with satisfaction, "but he thought we were rats."

"Are there rats?" said Laura.

"I should think."

"Can't we tell him we're here?" she pleaded. There was no point to this hiding.

"Shh," said Barty. The cowman was at the door again. He came into view carrying a bucket in each hand. One he carried over to the cow and set down beside her. Immediately they heard her suck noisily from it. They heard him slap her flank and speak softly to her. Then he stooped, looking intently down into the straw with his arms braced on his knees. Laura who had been so sure that the calf was alive felt her heart fail for it again. After a minute or two he straightened up and taking the other bucket emptied it into a trough by the door. They heard its contents, half solid half liquid, slide and fall. "It's for the pigs," whispered Barty. The cowman went to the door and whistled and a moment later the two great pigs came trotting into the barn. They began to suck up their food more noisily than the cow had done. The cowman took down his lantern and went outside.

"Can we go now?" whispered Laura.

Barty started to rise. Then he flattened himself onto the hay again. She felt his body stiffen against hers. He was listening. She too heard the sound grate against the base of the wall at the back of the barn. A bigger sound than rats. She looked towards it. One of the pale chinks of light grew suddenly and then vanished. Someone was climbing through the gap. She had not known she could lie so still. A boy. Bigger than Barty or smaller? It was hard to tell in the uncertain light. He began to move warily out onto the floor of the barn. Laura watched him through the straw. The small hairs on the back of her neck crept with hostility.

The boy had a stick in his hand. He went fearlessly over to the pigs and struck them on the back with it. The pigs jolted away from the trough snorting crossly. When they had gone the boy bent over the trough and looked inside it. He stretched out his arm and reached down into it. Then he called over his shoulder quite audibly. The sound took on no shape of any word in Laura's ear. Only she thought dully: There are to be more of them. She could hear Barty breathing quick and light beside her.

Another shape climbed through the gap. A girl. Laura made out her skirt when she moved and saw her turn back to the gap and pull through it a little boy. She steadied him on his feet and then pulled him roughly after her to the trough. The bigger boy caught him up and held him sprawling over the trough's edge. That's all, thought Laura. There aren't any more. She watched the girl. She too leant over the trough. Then she straightened and raised her arms to her face. There was so little light to see by that Laura, staring over the edge of the hay, received the confused and frightened impression that she was silently tearing at her mouth with her hands.

She heard the hay by her ear rustle. Barty was moving, groping in his pocket. He sat up suddenly and flung the little wizened apple straight and hard at the trough.

They did not even look about them to see what it was or where it had come from. They fled in an instant, without a sound, back through the gap in the wall. There was a second's pause while it was blocked again, a faint sound of running feet. Laura did not wait to listen. She was sliding down the stack. Barty hung above her kicking hay into her eyes. Her feet touched the ground. She ran to the door and forced herself through it. Outside in the muddy yard Barty ran past her without a word. Only when they were clear of the orchard and close to the lighted windows did they stop. They stood facing each other, panting and staring angrily.

"You could have waited," said Laura.

"You don't run fast enough."

"Perhaps I wasn't as scared as you."

"I wasn't scared."

She wanted to make him angry. She had it in her power within seconds to taunt him into a rage. Some shocked and frightened part of her wanted to do that, but at the back of her mind she knew that they must shortly appear before their aunt. Barty's rages could be terrible in their effects and last for hours. Instead she said with an odd little laugh she had not intended, "What were they doing?"

"Eating, of course." He looked at the ground as if he were embarrassed.

"Pig food?" said Laura incredulously. Yet she had seen it with her own eyes.

He made a mocking noise as if he might be sick. Then he laughed.

"It isn't funny," said Laura sharply. "It was stealing."

"Only from the pigs." He began to laugh again.

"You're never to go there again. Do you hear? You're not to."

"I'll go if I like."

"But you can't like *them*."

"They're not the sort you like or dislike," said Barty. "They were nothing but beggar children."

"You're horrid," cried Laura, outraged at his reasonableness. "I think you're horrid." To her surprise she began to cry, and ran towards the house rubbing at her face with a fold of her cloak, knowing that she must stop crying before she went in. "I never wanted to go," she said fiercely to herself. "I never wanted to come here at all." When that girl had seemed to hurt her face, that had been eating. It was horrid. They ate like that because they were horrid. They didn't know how to eat like people.

She tore at the thought and tried to throw it away, but no construction of rage and tears could hide its true nature. She knew quite well that they ate that way because they were hungry, and that, to do her credit, was at least in part why she wept.

CHAPTER THREE

In the house it was dinner time. "Here, you'll catch it and so shall I," said Amy tartly. "She has her friend here, and Master Henry come home and wanting his dinner." Through the scullery door they could see the kitchen full of steam. At the stove the village girl that came in by day clattered iron pans in a kind of frenzy.

"Quick now," urged Amy. Laura knelt on the stone flags of the scullery, intently picking straw from Barty's jacket while Amy battered at his hair with a brush. Barty pressed down the insides of his pockets with his clenched fists and scowled. He did nothing to help.

"Quick now, your hands." Hard and painfully she gripped first Laura's hands and then Barty's in one of her own and held them in a bunch while she pumped cold water over them at the scullery sink.

"Now your faces." Obediently they rubbed their wet cold hands over their eyes and cheeks. Then Amy set upon them each with a rough towel scrubbing mercilessly at their cheeks and at Barty's neck, even twisting the corner of it into his ears. It was like an attack. He hated it, but Laura felt grateful for the cold smarting cleanliness of her hands and face. The warmth of the kitchen and the smell of meat wrapped her like a blanket. Oh, it could not be. It could not be, she thought. It was almost a relief to fear her aunt's displeasure.

At last they were freed and pushed through the kitchen door into the passage. From behind the parlour door voices came in a murmur. Laura turned the handle with her cold hand and felt the damp woollen wristband of her dress gall her wrist. When she began to open the door the voices stopped.

There was a fresh white cloth on the table, stiff and sharply creased from folding. Aunt Bolinger sat as she had at breakfast, but with her chair pushed back so that she might the better speak to a small woman in a cap, who sat beside her regarding her with an eye as timidly bright and restless as some small rodent's. Uncle Bolinger stood in front of the fire, his boots astride, his coat tails looped over his arms. "Well," he said in a loud voice, poking his heavy head towards them. "Well, what do you think there is for dinner then? Who can guess?" He did not smile but as he spoke so especially to them Laura thought that he meant to be merry.

"Lamb," said Barty promptly. The whole house smelt of it.

"Lamb, *sir*," corrected his aunt from the table. "Come and say good evening to your cousin."

The tall young man, Henry, their cousin, was leaning over the back of the chair next to his mother. Now he straightened up and drew back the chair next to him,

31

saying to Laura, "Come. Come sit here."

"You've no cause to dance attendance on her," said his mother. "She's not apologised to my friend for being late."

"I am most sorry," said Laura to the little woman, who seemed to think it wise to say nothing but nodded and beamed placatingly all around her.

"This is my friend, Miss Lawton," said Aunt Bolinger.

"How do you do?" said Laura.

"Very well indeed, thank you, my dear."

Laura thought it safe then to sit down. She beckoned to Barty to sit beside her, and smiled shyly at her cousin, without yet looking fully at him.

"Well," said Uncle Bolinger heartily, twirling his coat tails with the fire glowing between his legs. "What did you find to do with yourselves all afternoon?"

The aunt's voice cut flatly across his. "Where have you been?" It was her they must answer. Laura said nothing.

Barty said, "Outside."

For a certainty she would say, "Outside where?", but she said instead, "You should say, 'Outside, Aunt.'"

It was a double relief, for now they had a name to call her by. *Aunt* had a stern sound to it, yet it did not deny the kinship. It would do very well. "Will you not come to the table, Mr Bolinger?" she now said. "We should not have to wait many minutes more."

They were now all seated to table. Laura found that by looking sideways in quick little glances she could see her Cousin Henry's face in profile against dark heavy curtains. She thought him sadly plain, his nose too long, his mouth altogether too wide for any nobility of expression. He was far older than she had imagined— twenty-one perhaps or even twenty-two—quite a grown man. Indeed Mama had told her that he was reading for Holy Orders, but then in the next breath she had called him "My sister's child, Keziah's boy," until Laura had hoped against reason that here might be a friend and equal. Clearly he was beyond that, yet young enough still for her to wonder how old he was. Each separate year a distinct territory, she would have liked to know exactly how far away he stood.

Now he turned to them and smiled. "Do you think you will like it here?" Barty smiled cautiously back at him and hunched his shoulders to his ears.

"What sort of an answer is that?" said Aunt Bolinger.

"Yes, thank you, Cousin Henry," said Laura quickly. How his smile had altered his face. The long line of his mouth had turned slowly upward with an expression of great sweetness as if he drew from some quiet source of inner pleasure quite preserved from his surroundings. Laura thought that she had really seen him now and liked him even better than at first.

Her aunt was saying crossly, "He should answer for himself."

"Oh let them be," said Uncle Bolinger thumping on the table with his napkin and almost shouting. Laura stared down at her own napkin. Could they be about to quarrel when the servants might at any moment enter the room? Did they always speak like this to one another?

At that moment boots did clatter in the hall. The

33

door swung open and Amy entered backwards carrying a heavy covered platter and followed by the girl from the village, anxiously carrying a tray of crockery. The food was set upon the table. At a sign from his mother Henry said a grace.

"Ah," said Uncle Bolinger. "This is what we've waited for." He adjusted his napkin and moved his knife and fork about on the cloth. Amy leant across the table to lift the heavy metal lid on which the steam flushed and faded. Her kitchen-smell of sweat and carbolic soap mingled with the warm smell of the lamb. Aunt Bolinger rose to carve.

"For all your fancy manservants and Halls," she said in a gratified voice, "you'll not have tasted sweeter meat than this since you went away to Oxford." Her displeasure was quite gone.

Freed from it, Laura sat with her hands folded and pressed between her knees. The warm room seemed to loose its hold of her. She smelt the barn, and felt the lining of her throat begin to swell. She wondered if she would be able to swallow the meat when it was set in front of her. She did not want it. When Barty was quite a small boy he had discovered the true origin of meat and seeing it on his plate would earnestly ask his mother, "Did it have eyes?" She had not been able to eat then. But after a while he had stopped asking and never seemed to worry about it since. Nor had she until now. She did not know why. She stared at the glistening roast, perplexed at her own feelings.

Now Miss Lawton with a quick glance from side to side ventured into the conversation. "It is a pity that the children could not have paid their visit in the summer months when it is so pretty in the fields and lanes."

Aunt Bolinger said, "We have not yet been told when they go."

"We are not staying very long," said Barty in a high anxious voice. He should not have said it in that way. They would think him rude. His aunt slowly lowered her carving tools and lifted her eyebrows at him.

"Is it not good enough for you then?"

"Oh, he did not mean that," said Laura. Her eyes began to smart with tears. It was wrong of her so to entrap and misinterpret him.

Henry said soothingly, "Mother, of course he did not, and if they are obliged to stay after I have gone back to Oxford, they will be company for you."

"They will that," said his mother dryly as if company were something she were well enough without. "Ah well," she added handing around the plates, "it was the least I could do for poor Lottie."

To Laura's surprise, her cousin turned to her and began to speak rapidly, almost stammering. "I remember your mother so distinctly. I was just a little boy, but I am sure she wore a flowered bonnet that looked very pretty to me. She gave me a marzipan and led me out by the hand for a walk and all the time she talked to me as if I were a person of quite her own age. I am sure any child would be drawn to her at once. You must ask her if she remembers that day." He was quite flushed when he stopped. Laura smiled at him fully and openly. She felt it was very good of him to have spoken so, and guessed obscurely that to do so had been an act of courage.

For the rest of the meal she continued to snatch swift looks at him, the better to come to terms with his plainness. Indeed each time she looked his homely face seemed to soften and further yield to the true picture she was making of him in her mind until it seemed almost transformed, as it often was in truth, by the sweetness of his smile.

I am his cousin, she thought solemnly. I always shall be. She began to think of all the ways she might be useful to him, all the ways her mother was useful to her father. She was thinking in terms of lifelong assistance, yet a moment before she had wondered how she could endure to stay in this house to the extent of another day. To her relief she suddenly felt hungry again.

Barty, too, sensed Henry's good will and now leant over to him and said, "Why does she call Mama poor when she is not poor?"

This time it was Miss Lawton who came to the rescue. "Hush, Barty. Your aunt did not mean that she was poor in *that* sense. It is only that your dear mama and papa must work so very hard for the poor sick people in the city, and you have come here so as not to hinder—not, dears, that you would be a hindrance; I am sure you would be a good sweet help to them, but it would never do for you yourselves to fall ill and be a worry to them at this time. So your kind aunt has had you out to the country where the air is pure . . . ." Here, seeing Aunt Bolinger's ironic eye upon her, her voice took fright and turned tail between her lips which hastily shut upon it.

Laura said, "As soon as the cholera goes away they

will send for us again."

"Of course," said Uncle Bolinger, with his loaded fork poised in the air. "Of course they will and in the meantime we must find things for you to do." He began shifting in his chair as if actually preparing then and there for some activity.

His wife frowned at him. "There's no shortage of things to do," she said to Henry. "Do you ever see me idle?" He smiled at her, with such open affection that Laura thought: Why, he likes her, and felt surprised. A moment later when suety pudding had been set steaming before them she heard her cousin draw in his breath and say a little hesitantly, "I must walk over to the vicarage tomorrow. I could take the children with me. The old people would so like to see them."

"There is no need for that," said his mother. "Miss Lawton and I shall be going in any case in the afternoon to attend a meeting of the Ladies' Committee. Laura may come with us as she sews so neatly and you if you wish may accompany us." She added in a wintry tone, "It is the old people you are going to see, of course."

He answered carelessly, "I suppose Miss Roylance may be there."

"I wonder they have her to live with them," said Aunt Bolinger. There was a pause.

Oh, what is this now? thought Laura. Clearly it was of some significance to them, but meaningless to her. Cousin Henry sat patiently smiling at his hands, setting up no resistance.

His mother turned instead to Miss Lawton whose eyes, once caught, followed her nervously. "When I was

37

a girl, parson did not hob-nob with the schoolmistress outside what you might call business, the catechism and that."

Laura sensed this was no idle conversation, but knew with relief that she and Barty no longer figured in it. She ate her pudding very slowly, wondering who these people might be.

She heard her Cousin Henry say mildly, "Mother, you know they are happy to have her living there."

"Aye, and they're happy enough to have you come calling so often."

"Now, Mother . . ."

"Well, they'll not want her on their hands forever. She's nothing but her genteel manners to her name and we've a sight more."

"But Mother, if I'm to have the curacy next year and be of any help to Mr Armitage, I must see him. I must go to the vicarage and if Miss Roylance is there . . ."

"We all know she is there," interrupted his mother. "But where is she *from* is what I should like to know."

Miss Lawton made a swift forward gesture with her little hands and began eagerly to supply again information that all of them knew. "Her parents are dead. Her father, they say, was an officer, killed in India. I believe her mother was in sadly reduced circumstances and at her death Miss Roylance was taken in by an aunt in Balham," here she dropped her voice, "as little more than a servant."

"Fair enough," remarked Aunt Bolinger.

"Still," pursued Miss Lawton, "although we may presume that her father was no more than an Indian officer, an officer is an officer, is he not, dear?" She stretched open her eyes. "They say he was a major, but then perhaps things are very different out there and there is less significance in it."

"Oh," said Aunt Bolinger carelessly, "I daresay he's been much promoted since he fell. It's often the way, is it not, Miss Lawton? They'll give him the regiment in another year or so, I shouldn't wonder." All the time that she spoke she enquired silently of each of them, with a lift of her eyes and a gesture of the spoon, if they would care for more pudding, so that Laura felt unhappily that by murmuring, "Yes please," and passing along her plate she had joined against Henry in mocking the poor dead soldier.

Henry said, "You know this is all nonsense, Mother." He gave an awkward little laugh, part amused, part placating, partly, it seemed to Laura, in some hope that he might turn the edge of his mother's words and make them mean something different. "I have no choice but to visit Mr Armitage. It means much to all of us that I should have the curacy."

Aunt Bolinger said nothing. It seemed that this was an unanswerable argument. Miss Lawton, as if trained to cover her friend's set-backs, said, "I hear there is to be a little calf soon." She beamed watchfully about her. "When I was a little girl, Laura, I was sometimes allowed to feed the calf. At least I believe I was. I know I very much wanted to."

"I will not have a niece of mine smelling of the byre," said Aunt Bolinger, rising with dignity from the table. "We pay a man to feed the calf."

"That is true, dear," said Miss Lawton hurrying after her. "There really is no need to feed the calf. Still they are such dear little things."

"I daresay it will carve well enough when the time comes," said Aunt Bolinger.

As they all crossed the passage into the drawing room Barty said, "But may we go and see it? In a day or two? When it's a little bigger?"

Laura stared at him in admiration. Really there had been no need at all to lie.

CHAPTER FOUR

*In the attics the children woke one by one, cold, their
limbs and bodies cramped against one another: James
Andrews, William Andrews, William Derbyshire—all in a
bed. The rats racketed in the thin partitions between the
attics. It was time to get up. Between the boards nailed
over the window the grey winter light seeped and lay
along the sloping walls like a film of dirt.*

*James was six. He knew he was awake because he was
hungry but he could not see. It frightened him to wake
like that. He felt along the rough crust of his lashes. "I
can't open them," he said. "Do my eyes, Will." He lay
still and felt his brother's body curl around him. He felt
the rough shirt tail rub at his eyelids, first one free, then
the other.*

*"Get up quick and piddle," said his brother, "or
you'll wet." He ran to the round wooden tub set
between the beds in the attic and lifted his shirt. He
wasn't the first. Steam rose off it. The tub stank.*

*Thomas Deighton, the big boy, came through the
door carrying the tub from the next attic. Because he*

41

was big he must carry it down and empty it into the
sewer and then rinse it at the pump and fill it with
water. Then he carried it back up the stairs and began to
scrub the floorboards between the beds. He never spoke.
Jamie thought: If I get big they'll make me do that.
Stinking tub. But he wouldn't. He'd get round it
somehow. Will would get him out of it.

The wall of the attics, the wall of the house, the wall
of the yard, the narrow space between, and then the
garden wall and the wall of the Bolingers' house. Within
it Laura lay for a while hoarding her slight store of
warmth before she must get out into the cold room and
dress herself. The smooth clear passage of sleep made
her look back in wonder at her disgust and fright the
night before in the barn. She had even cried. Poor
children, she thought, comforting herself in the narrow
bed. Poor children. But the pain of seeing them had
passed. Still she would never go back to the barn again.
Not in the dark. Not ever, if Barty would let her be.
Only if the calf were alive—and now in the morning it
seemed again that it might be—would she go. But never
alone, never in the dark.

As she left the room and crossed the landing, it
seemed to Laura that she could hear a sound of
shouting: not of one voice shouting to another, but
many voices, high, thin and aimless, outside the house.
She turned the handle of the storeroom door and went
inside, shutting it quickly behind her. She went to the
window and looking down towards the noise saw a sight
as astonishing to her as a fall of snow. The yard beyond

the orchard wall that yesterday had lain so empty was filled with children. She had never seen so many children together before. Wisps of white breath rose from their mouths and vanished. Their shouting was scarcely stronger. Laura laid her arm against the cold window and rested her head against it. It seemed to her that the sound they made was quite inadequate for all those people. She wanted to open the window so that the sound might be strengthened. But the thought that they might see her and that all those faces might turn up towards her, shouting, made her reach for her handkerchief. Using a little spit she carefully wiped one of the panes free of dust and stared again down at the horde of children. She had seen at once, as with the solitary little girl, by the ill-kempt or shaven outlines of their heads, by the ungainly shape of their clothes, that they too were poor people's children. But so many! Where had they come from? In one village there could not be so many poor children. Maybe it's a school, thought Laura. But children like that did not go to school.

She began to search among the multitude for the girl who had skipped, but nowhere in all that crowd could she see a swinging rope. There was scarcely room. Now her eyes began to single out this child and that. Three little girls, their pinafores stretched over their knees, squatted by a puddle to shape pies. A little boy far smaller than Barty sullenly dragged behind him an old boot on a length of string and there was a boy Barty's size running by the wall and striking at it again and again as he ran with a stick. With each blow he executed a curious joyless caper. Now a long line of taller girls with their arms about each other's waists began to sway and waver across the yard, but they scarcely made progress. Again and again they collided with groups of boys elbowing along with hands in pockets, scuffing the dirt with their boots, and must make arches with their arms to let them through, or break off and struggle to join again. At least they tried, thought Laura. All along the base of the walls and buildings children sat with their shoulders huddled together, their arms wrapped about them for warmth, their heads leaning back, their faces turned listlessly towards the sun. They should get up and play, thought Laura impatiently. Someone's sure to make them go inside soon. They will have wasted their time. Yet the sight interested Laura profoundly. She kept her face close to the glass and several times had to use her handkerchief again to rub it clear of her cloudy breath. Why ever had no one mentioned this place?

At breakfast she would have liked to have asked who those children were, but she did not. Over the tapping of little bone spoons on eggshells, the clink of cups and plates, Laura could still hear the thin sound of shouting. She looked at her aunt's settled features, at Uncle Bolinger's red cheeks active over toast and Cousin Henry's face, gentle, remote, visiting, it seemed to Laura, in some other place. It must be that they could not hear. A minute later she thought she heard the sound of a distant handbell. The shouting stopped. Laura looked again from one face to another. They showed no awareness of the sound or the silence. Barty's face hung over his plate sheltered by his hair. Perhaps he had heard. And the others had all heard.

They must have done, but for some reason the sound was as inappropriate here as the cries of the cow.

The wall of this house, the garden wall, the space between, and then the other where the children stood to breakfast in long rows, their shoulders touching: pottage of flour, milk, water and salt, in sufficient proportions.

When the plates were cleared away into the scullery, Laura followed Amy from room to room gathering the spent lamps onto a tray. She said cautiously, "Are there any children here I might play with?"

Amy set out ahead of her carrying the tray to the kitchen. "None I know of," she said. "Parson never married and Dr Parrot's girl's away at boarding school."

She was so tiny. Walking behind her you might think she was a child herself had she not been so very stiff, like a wooden doll. "But *any* child?" insisted Laura.

"What would you mean by any child, Miss Laura?" Amy had set the tray on the kitchen table and already had begun to lift off the clouded glass mantles of the lamps, but she stopped to look steadily at Laura with her head tilted stiffly to one side.

"Can I trim them?" said Barty.

She did not shift her eyes from Laura but pushed the scissors towards him. Laura lowered her eyes and slid her fingers around a candle blunting the sharp edge of the melted wax. She shrugged her shoulders.

"I thought I heard some voices. That was all."

"They're on the far side of the wall," said Barty.

"And what would you know about the far side of the

wall?"

"I could hear them," he said carelessly. "It's a school or something."

"Is it a school?" said Laura quickly.

"You might call it that."

The serving girl came to the scullery door, twisting her hands in her sacking apron. "So they found out about Drouet's place already," she said.

Amy rubbed mechanically at the brass lampstand.

"What are you going to tell them?" said the girl in an interested gossiping voice.

"That will do," said Amy.

"If you wouldn't call it a school, what would you call it?" said Barty.

"There's some calls it a baby farm," said Amy, looking not at them now but obliquely down at the brass lamp which her hands continued to rub long past cleanliness.

"But they weren't babies," said Laura. "Some of them were as big as I am."

"You saw them then," said Amy looking at her, quick as a cat. "You didn't just hear them. How would you have managed to see them then?"

"From the storeroom window," said Laura in a low voice. She had meant no harm but she felt as if she had done wrong.

"What's a baby farm?" said Barty.

Amy poked her face close to his and said in a pretended threat, "A place where they put children nobody wants."

Barty laughed, but Laura could not make light of it.

"Are their parents dead?"

"Perhaps. Perhaps not."

"But if their parents are alive, somebody wants them."

"Their parents are paupers, miss," said the village girl and went back to the scullery as if that were an end to it. They heard the sound of the plates.

Laura would not let the matter drop.

"But why are there so many poor people in this village?"

"Oh they're not from here. They're from all the rookeries of London. It's nothing to do with this village. Drouet's lot don't come under Vicar nor vestry. They've been wished on us by the government as ought to have known better in a free country, without so much as a by-your-leave."

"But why is it called a farm?" persisted Barty.

"It might be because he treats them like animals, and then again it might not. It's not for me to say or you to ask." And Amy snapped her long wrinkled upper lip onto her straight thin lower one, as if after a lifetime of practise of keeping her own counsel.

Like animals, Barty thought. Is that good or bad? He had always regretted not being an animal. When he was small he would rub at the down on his arms and pray that it might be the first sign of fur. He had studied his hands and seeing the faint domes of flesh on the tips of his fingers had thought with a surge of hope that claws might be growing. Now he had more or less given up hope. But Laura was not so easily distracted. For all the questions and answers she felt as mystified as before.

47

But she could ask her Cousin Henry. She had perfect faith that he would tell her.

After the midday meal, preparations began at once for the visit to the vicarage. Laura went up to her room. She went to the blotched mirror and combed out the top of her hair. Then she smoothed her pinafore, found a clean handkerchief, took her cloak from its peg and wrapped it round her. As she passed the storeroom door she tried the handle. It was locked. Amy, after she told her about those children, must have come especially and locked them away from her sight. Why? thought Laura. She felt that something had been taken from her. Not a pleasant thing perhaps but something necessary, that had needed more time. Was that how she felt? Or had she only an uncomfortable sense of being caught out in some wrong when she had meant none. And now there was nothing to be done for it.

She went slowly downstairs to where Henry and her aunt waited in the hall. "Where's Barty?" she said.

"I'm not taking him to a sewing party at the vicarage," said her aunt. "He must make his own amusements." And taking Henry's arm and giving Laura her workbag she set out through the front door.

Laura had not yet been on this side of the house in daylight. The bleak winter distances, the uncertain half lights of the orchard and the barn had seemed the landscape in which the house was set. From here it seemed quite another place. The day was cold and clear. The sharp wind seemed to blow light across the surface of things, from branch to branch of the black stiffly moving trees, racing across the puddles and cart ruts.

The grass by the roadside was a brilliant green.

She saw now that her aunt's house lay on the corner of a cross-roads. The wide muddy road across which they picked their way was so printed by wheels and horse shoes that it could only be the London Road on which they had arrived after dark. The narrower road that cut across it became a village street where the small clapboard shops and cottages huddled together for support and comfort as if the turnpike traffic from the outer world was little to be trusted. Laura looked back at the proud frontage of her aunt's house, and then with a quickening of excitement she looked for the house that must lie in front of the yardful of children. There to one side was the pub with its yard and its sign and its two great lamps. To the other side was a fine old house, handsomer even than her aunt's, with iron railings and a wrought-iron gate. Stone steps climbed up to the door and, above, tall windows stood in ranks flashing white in the sunlight. As she looked an upstairs sash slid open and a maidservant leant out and flapped a mat. I am mistaken, thought Laura. Yet there to one side was the pub, to the other this fine house. The yard must stretch behind it. She pulled timidly at her aunt's arm, and said, "For whom do we do our sewing, Aunt?"

Her aunt said briefly, "For charity."

They had turned now into the village street. Ahead of them the church spire, sharp and grey, rose among naked branches. By the gate of a garden Laura saw the slight figure of Miss Lawton turning her bonneted head this way and that as if there were no limit to the directions from which they might appear. When Miss

Lawton saw them she lifted both her hands in what seemed a gesture of astonishment and came hurrying forward. "I was afraid we might be late. It would never do to arrive after Mrs Rees-Goring."

"We are not late in the least," said Aunt Bolinger. "It is you who fuss."

"Well that's a mercy then," said Miss Lawton cheerfully. "Is it not a pretty village, Laura? You will not have seen the church yet. It is a new church, dear, and very well appointed. Gas light and an organ. Has your father the same? We are very proud of it, being raised by public subscription."

"It is not very new," said Aunt Bolinger.

"Oh but most churches are so very old and so very inconvenient. And it does not seem long since I came with my father, the late physician, to attend the consecration. We waited, you know, at the church gates to see the arrival of the bishop and all the gentry and poor old Dr Ravensgill to greet them, who as you may know, died of an apoplexy that very evening after serving tea to the bishop at the vicarage, the excitements of the day being too much for him. And yet as he handed down the bishop, and I can see it as I pass these gates, the thought cannot have entered his head. It was altogether a memorable occasion. You were a boy, Henry, but you cannot fail to remember it."

Does he remember? thought Laura looking at her cousin. She was not at all sure that he did. Her aunt had released her son's arm and fallen into step with Miss Lawton, so that Henry had walked hurriedly forward and seemed quite unaware that he was being appealed

50

to. Laura quickened her pace and found she had almost
to run to come up with him. She hoped it had not been
noticed, but indeed he did not seem to notice her at all.
He strode and she hurried beside him in silence. At last
she said, "Where are we going?" She seemed to feel each
separate word pass through her mouth. Her voice
sounded quite unlike itself; the question quite foolish,
forced out of the hard obligation to speak. Yet she had
actually wanted the opportunity to speak with him
alone and, remembering that, she said in a rush, when he
had hardly had a chance to say that the vicarage was just
behind the church, "Who are the children in the house
next door?"

She watched him intently as she asked, fearing that
his answer might slip by without solving anything.
Cousin Henry frowned slightly as if he must choose his
words. "I believe it is some kind of a school."

But he must know, thought Laura. She said timidly,
"They did not look the sort of children that go to school."
Then, when he did not answer, "Is it a charity school?"

"Yes," said her cousin abruptly, "I suppose charity
comes into it somewhere."

What she had said had not interested him at all.
Perhaps she had sounded foolish; perhaps she did not
know what sorts of children went to school and what
did not. He did not attend to her. Now they were
walking past the new wrought-iron gates of the modern
church and she felt him quicken his step and saw him
glance back impatiently at the slow figures of his
mother and Miss Lawton. He wanted to be there. He
wanted the walk to be over.

CHAPTER FIVE

Laura, entering the vicarage parlour behind her aunt, knew right away that she liked it here. The warm air smelt pleasantly of the smouldering logs in the fireplace. The sparse delicate furniture seemed to have been set in place long ago. Books lined the walls and stood in orderly piles on little tables. In a chair, by the side of the fire, sat an old woman wrapped in a grey shawl. She was sorting embroidery wools in a box on her lap.

A table covered with a fresh cloth was set in the window where the sun fell upon it. Bending over it Laura saw a slight young woman with the sun alive in her thick bright hair, arranging piles of little garments and extra thimbles and pincushions as if she were setting out a game.

The old lady said slowly and contentedly, "Margaret, someone has come and look she has brought a child." Her eyes did not touch at all on Aunt Bolinger or Miss Lawton, but went straight to Laura. She smiled and held out her hands which shook as she held them there so that the delicate rings on her fingers rattled. Laura took them quickly as she knew she was meant to do and stayed holding the old lady's hands, smiling shyly at her.

"You have come to see me, child," said Miss Armitage in her slow wondering voice. "I am rather vague today and my cap I fear is very vague." She let go of Laura's hands and began absorbedly to tuck the soft escaped strands of yellow-white hair up under the rim of her cap. The young woman had come forward quickly from the table and with a slight exchange of greeting with Aunt Bolinger and Miss Lawton leant over the back of the chair and settled the cap, kissing the old lady and saying, "There, my dear, you look quite bobbish."

Laura saw that she was a small person, delicately formed as a child, only something cautious and saddened in her eyes was entirely unchildlike. She must be the schoolmistress they had talked about, but no one had mentioned that she was young, or that her hair was red. For a moment her steady grey eyes rested on Laura appraisingly, but kindly too, so that Laura who hated to be stared at found she did not mind. Then Miss Roylance smiled and touched her lightly on the shoulder, and motioned her to sit on a little stool at Miss Armitage's feet.

"Will Mrs Rees-Goring be present?" Miss Lawton asked the schoolmistress eagerly.

"We expect her."

"And where is she to sit?"

"Why, where she chooses," said Miss Roylance with a laugh, returning to busy herself at the table. Miss Lawton and Aunt Bolinger exchanged a look. She did not laugh unkindly though, thought Laura.

"I should think," Miss Lawton went on, indicating an armchair somewhat more substantial than the rest, "that she would choose to sit there. Do not you, dear? I have always admired the Berlin-work so. Your work, I'm sure Miss Armitage," she called across to the old lady, adding significantly behind her mitten, "in happier days." She settled quickly into the chair next to it.

Miss Armitage paid no attention. She laid the little skeins of wool neatly side by side in the box and smiled at the colours. When the old lady looked enquiringly at Laura, Laura knew to touch her favourite one, a dark red. That was a good choice. It was taken out and put at the head of the row.

The maid then came in to announce that Mrs Rees-Goring had indeed arrived, and immediately a broad handsome lady pressed smiling through the door, her wide silk skirts whispering about her like a crowd of awed attendants. The ladies noticed at once that the silk was of an indefinable blend of mauve and grey. To Laura, her skirts and her flimsy shawl, her lacy cap and creamy skin, gave an impression of infinite but untouchable softness. She was a lady and Laura need not exactly *like* her, only she must be very polite.

When Miss Armitage made move to rise, Mrs Rees-Goring graciously took her hand and patted it, saying sweetly, "No, no, dear Miss Armitage, but you are not to stir out of your chair for me. How very well you are looking and how is the Vicar?"

Miss Armitage regarded her with little interest, but she had understood, for a moment later she answered in her slow distinct voice, "He is very taken up with the excavations at Nineveh, but perhaps he will join us presently."

Mrs Rees-Goring's smile did not falter. Merely it floated on to Laura as she did her curtsy. Momentarily the soft hand touched Laura's cheek and the soft voice asked, "Whose child are you?"

"She is my niece," said Aunt Bolinger, "who is come to help us," and to Laura's surprise she performed if not a curtsy, a definite lessening of erectness that admitted some deference.

Miss Lawton's curtsy was graceless but more absolute. When she had recovered from it she darted behind the Berlin-work chair and began edging it forward.

Mrs Rees-Goring smiled and nodded to the ladies with impartial sweetness. Everyone was silent while she settled herself as had been intended, and shook from her arms her shawl, her workbag and her reticule. "There," she said. "Now . . . and how are my doughty workers progressing?"

Miss Lawton raised her hands to either side of her face in a kind of playful dismay. "Oh, my dear Mrs Rees-Goring, shall I ever be finished by Christmas? This petticoat is but half done and I declare a child needing seams this long has no business being at school at all."

"Courage," said Mrs Rees-Goring. "Courage. You have never failed me yet, Miss Lawton. You shall see. You shall be through before we part and then we must consider what we shall adventure upon in the new year." Miss Lawton beamed and bent at once to her task.

"And you, Mrs Bolinger? That sock is the second of

55

the pair?"

"The toe remains," said Aunt Bolinger, "but it will be finished within the hour."

"Good, good. And your little helper?"

"Laura will hem this cloak," she answered reaching a garment from the table. "Laura, come here where the light is good and start your work."

Laura was sad to leave Miss Armitage but she took her stool obediently and settled it in the patch of sunlight by her aunt's dark skirts.

"Have you a thimble, Laura?" asked Miss Roylance. Laura shook her head. Miss Roylance came and knelt beside her. She took Laura's hand and holding it up asked seriously, "Do you like a little one that perches on your finger?"

"Yes, please," said Laura shyly.

Miss Roylance smiled and said almost in a whisper, "I have a little one here. It was mine as a child, and I was especially fond of it. But now I am grown too big and I cannot wedge it on." She began to feel in the pocket at her waist and produced a silver thimble which she tried on Laura's middle finger. "There," she said, looking at Laura happily. "There, it is a perfect fit. You shall wear it whenever you come here." Liking passed between them. The thimble was a treasure shared.

Miss Roylance rose and taking her chair close to the window began to work with bent head at a grey wool mitten. Laura stole glances at her from time to time. She thought her very pretty with her little neck held so and her bright hair. Miss Roylance sat on the very edge of her chair as if at any moment something might be requested of her, yet she seemed to be quite apart from the others. How odd, Laura thought, that they paid no attention to her. She was far more interesting than they were. It was odd, too, how here Aunt Bolinger kept silent while Miss Lawton led the conversation with many references to "my father, the late physician," and even once, "my great uncle, the late rear admiral."

Laura had not yet come to feel any obligation to talk in company. Indeed it would be wrong to do so unless directly questioned, and here, to her relief, she was not. She heard the steady ceaseless rise and fall of women's talk but made no effort to distinguish the words from the other sounds in the room: the patter of bone needles, the settling of the fire.

The garment that had been given her, without explanation, was a grey woollen cape cut so small it must be intended for quite a little child. She bent over it, intent, amid her thoughts, on sewing it as quickly and neatly as she could, to win her aunt's approval and justify her coming here. Yet all the time she sewed she was aware of this pleasant room where the winter sun, warm within the window panes, awakened all the golds in the worn rugs and faded wallpaper. It was safe here. The tight caution that had possessed her since her arrival at her aunt's house, slept. Safe to take out and examine, as she sewed, the mysteries of the barn; here where they could not harm or frighten her. The calf had lived inside its mother. And she? Had she? How strange. And could she ever be so hungry that she would cram rotting food into her mouth, wanting it? And who was to care for that child skipping in the yard and all those other children whose parents had cast them off? And she? And she?

Her hand with the little thimble rose and fell. The stitches lay in the cloth as private as handwriting, hers, to be given away to someone of whom she knew nothing. For charity. Some charity child. The good cloth spread a patch of warmth on her knee and it pleased her to think that gift of warmth would be passed on to the other poor cold child. But the poor child would not stay a shadow. It took on the shape of a girl skipping in the wind.

When she had finished she carried the cape over to the chair by the window. Silently Miss Roylance took it from her hands and held it up to the light to inspect the hemming. "Yes," she said smiling directly at Laura. "It is well done. Thank you, Laura."

Laura smiled back, held in the warmth of acceptance, heedless of the other ladies. She said, "Is it to go to the children that live next door to my aunt?" She had not spoken loudly and only to Miss Roylance, but at that moment Miss Lawton had paused in her recollections and the words carried into a quiet room.

Aunt Bolinger said angrily, "You'll not catch me sewing for the likes of them in a hurry."

"These are for our own village children, Laura," said Mrs Rees-Goring. "Had you not been told? Those Miss Roylance has charge of in the charity school. Mr Rees-Goring and I shall ourselves present them at a tea at the manor house on Christmas day."

Laura felt the blood crowd to her face. She had asked a foolish question. She wished all the more that she had kept silent when her aunt leant towards her and enquired coldly, "What made you think it might be for those other children?"

She had to stand in front of them all and say in a low unsteady voice, "I saw, out of the window, a little girl skipping in the yard, and she had nothing warm to wear. I thought perhaps the clothes were for those children." She was nearly in tears, but no one was angry with her.

Mrs Rees-Goring said, "Why, bless the child. She has been well brought up to charitable thoughts, has she not, ladies?" There was a gentle murmur and if Aunt Bolinger's straight lips did not move with it, nor did they dare open in opposition to Mrs Rees-Goring.

Miss Lawton said, "Laura dear, you are not to be concerned about those children. They are nothing to do with this village. They are all from other parishes. Slum parishes in London. It is very sad for them, poor things, that their parents are paupers, but nothing you or I could do could alter that, now could it? So they are truly no concern of ours."

Laura was aware that Miss Roylance had risen to her feet before she heard Miss Armitage. The old lady's voice seemed to fill the room. "Oh, but I am concerned for those children. For their souls and bodies, I am most concerned." She moved impulsively as if trying to rise to her feet and scattered the little box of wools on to the floor.

Miss Roylance moved quickly across the room, but before she could reach her, Miss Armitage had sunk back in her chair looking about her in confusion, seeming to know neither from where her voice had come nor whence it had gone. She felt for her wools on her lap and, finding them missing, she began to search agitatedly down the sides of her chair. Miss Roylance turned and motioned to Laura to pick them up, and Laura was glad enough to be on her knees with her back to the cruel exchange of glances and shrugs that passed between the ladies. She knew she had caused it all by speaking when she should not have done. She gathered the skeins quickly into the box and laid them on Miss Armitage's knee. Miss Roylance knelt beside her, holding the old lady's hands in hers, stroking them gently with her thumbs, partly to soothe and partly, it seemed to Laura, she chafed them as if to keep something alive.

Kneeling as she did, Miss Roylance turned to face the watching ladies. Laura saw her straighten her neck and shoulders, saw the colour rise swiftly up her neck into her cheeks. "Mrs Rees-Goring," she said, "you asked for suggestions as to what sewing we might undertake in the new year. And the other evening Miss Armitage and I were talking—were we not? Do you remember?—about Mr Drouet's children and we thought that we might offer our services there."

Mrs Rees-Goring did not hasten to answer. She first set down her sewing, regarding Miss Roylance steadily. Then she appealed to the other ladies with her eyes. "Did I ask for suggestions?" she said mildly. "I was not aware that I had."

"Nor was I," said Miss Lawton.

"I'd be seen dead before I sew for the likes of them."

"One minute," said Mrs Rees-Goring. "Let me make

60

sure that I have not misunderstood you, Miss Roylance. Was it yours, or, as you say, Miss Armitage's suggestion that the Ladies' Committee should take to sewing for the pauper children in Mr Drouet's establishment?"

For a moment Miss Roylance looked anxiously to the old lady, but no help would come from there. "That we should offer," she said. "That we should make some contact with Mr Drouet."

"Have we any indication that he needs his sewing done?" said Mrs Rees-Goring. "Perhaps you have the courage to approach a man who is a stranger to you with such an offer, Miss Roylance?"

"I should be prepared to approach him," said Miss Roylance.

"Then you are a very daring young woman. I confess I should be too afraid that he might think me interfering."

An appreciative titter came from Miss Lawton.

"I should not call it interference," said Miss Roylance with her face red and held very high. "I should call it, as Miss Armitage does, a very justifiable concern."

"Those were not quite Miss Armitage's words." For the first time there glinted in her tone a cutting edge. "Still, no doubt you have a meaning of your own."

"I have. That we have a right, a duty, to know more of the conditions those children live under."

"We?" said Mrs Rees-Goring. "To whom do you ally yourself?"

"The village."

"Ah. You speak for the village? Have you, Miss Roylance, any indication that he maltreats his children?"

"There are stories in the village you may not have heard."

"Ah, my dear, you are very young but you should know enough to pay no heed at all to cottagers' tales. Why some years ago my sister in Norfolk was stopped by one of her people in the street." Here she paused and fetched up her knitting again and the ladies, sensing at once that the purpose of this coming anecdote was to guide them all back to safer ground, instantly followed suit. "A woman she had known all her life, distraught with weeping and crying out, 'Oh the children, the poor children!' And she, thinking this woman's own children were in some dreadful plight, said, 'Whatever is the matter?'

" 'Oh,' cries the woman, 'the Queen has said that every first born child in the land is to be slain. Whatever are we to do!' "

The ladies lowered their work in appreciation. They listened intently. For this tale was a precious item to be bartered for weeks to come, containing such popular components as the Queen, other people's deaths, and Mrs Rees-Goring's sister who was a lady of title.

Mrs Rees-Goring resumed, "So my sister reassured her as best she could that it was most unlikely and went on her way, only to have the same tale repeated to her in every cottage she entered. And would you believe it, in the end she traced the whole thing back to a report in the local paper that the Queen had had her eldest son vaccinated, and those ignorant people had twisted the information this way and that, until that is what they had convinced themselves. Would you credit it? In this age of progress!"

Aunt Bolinger clicked her tongue and Miss Lawton tittered incredulously. Their fingers sped as each tried to think of an anecdote to follow. But Miss Roylance had not done. She gently laid Miss Armitage's hands on the box of wool, and now she came over to the table and faced Mrs Rees-Goring directly.

"If I have not your support, might I at least approach as a private person—approach Mrs Drouet if you would rather?"

Mrs Rees-Goring glanced about her with exasperation. She said pointedly, "But you are not present with us as a private person. You are here solely because you are our schoolmistress. And as chairwoman of the Ladies' Committee I must expressly forbid you to take any such action." Then she paused and looked at Miss Roylance with no trace of a smile. "Of course if at any time you cease to be the schoolmistress then you would truly be a private person and might act as you wish."

There was silence then. Laura knew something had been said that had not been said. Miss Roylance did not answer but went back to her chair and bowed her head over her knitting. Mrs Rees-Goring said with a note of finality, "Mr Drouet has his own doctor resident at the asylum, and his own clergyman. Mr Rees-Goring looked into all that most particularly, Miss Roylance. I can assure you of that. The asylum is inspected regularly and without warning by the Guardians of the work-houses who send their children there. Besides that there is nothing we need to know about the place. One may or may not agree with the Poor Laws but no one can claim that they are not thorough in execution."

"Well it's a bad law when all's said and done," pronounced Aunt Bolinger. "They took our own poor from us, whom we knew well enough how to handle, without so much as a by-your-leave, but an increase on the rates, never fear. And that I'd not grudge had I any say on whom they chose to spend it. For who is to say if a man is deserving of charity or undeserving if they have not grown up with him in the same village?"

"Indeed they cannot," said Miss Lawton. "When I think of the stitching I put into the flannel nightshirts for the Benson children—plain felling of course in their circumstances, but as neatly done as for you, Mrs Rees-Goring. And not a stitch would we sew for Mary North, who as we all know drank. And now they are all herded off to Wandsworth Union like cattle with no discrimination."

"Well there was little enough to choose between them," said Aunt Bolinger. "But that's not to say they had the right to take our poor from us and fill the village with the scouring of the London slums. Not that one ever sees them except in church. I'll say that for him. He keeps them out of sight."

So it is all right, thought Laura. Papa was a Guardian of the poor. She knew how they managed the work-house. They weighed out the bread: so many ounces every day for each poor person, so many ounces of meat, and warm clean clothes and a bed.

"Yet they will die," Papa had said, setting down the heavy silver knife and fork so violently that the table shook and the glasses chimed together. The candle flames had flapped. "They will die rather than go in to those places." He had meant the workhouses. But if the place where the children were was like the workhouses, the Guardians inspected and weighed the bread. There must be enough to eat; there must be enough to wear. It must be all right, thought Laura.

The conversation did not recover. Silence had stretched beyond that indefinable moment when it becomes almost impossible to break. Everyone was relieved when tea was brought in, and Henry and the Reverend Mr Armitage joined the party. The sewing and knitting was put away and with it all thought of those troubling matters they had been discussing. Mrs Rees-Goring asked the Vicar about the finds at Nineveh.

Mr Armitage had taken the chair opposite his sister. "Ah," he said turning his bony head with its fine fringe of white hair towards Mrs Rees-Goring, "Margaret has been reading me the latest accounts. Alas, I tend to forget what she has read, but nowadays I find I cannot remember anything."

"And very convenient he finds it, too," said his sister inclining her head knowingly towards Henry.

"Yet," continued the Vicar, "the subject has great appeal. It is like the raising of the dead. So many questions. Why the intellect hankers after these assurances, I do not know."

Henry shifted his chair forward. He began to tell Mr Armitage about a letter one of his Oxford friends had received from his brother who was actually working on the site. All the time that he was speaking he kept glancing across at the window, quick stolen glances to where Miss Roylance sat with her hands braced lightly behind her on the chair. Her hair, escaping from the knot at the back of her neck, sprang and burnt against the window glass. I suppose he intends someday to marry her, thought Laura, watching. She felt no loss or jealousy. If anything the idea rather pleased her. She liked Miss Roylance so very much already.

Later, after they had walked home through the winter dusk, Aunt Bolinger stopped Laura at the foot of the stairs and tipping her head to one side, considered her shrewdly. "You have not spoken to any of those pauper children?"

Laura flushed and shook her head. Her aunt should have known she would not have done such a thing. She had seen them straightaway for what they were.

"Then what do you know about them?"

"I saw them from the storeroom window. I asked Amy who lived in that house, and she told me they were poor children."

Her aunt looked hard upon her, but contented herself with saying, "I'll not have your mother holding me to task for your picking up rough ways and rude speech while staying in my house, to say nothing of what else you might pick up. I suppose that Barty has not been speaking with them?"

"No, Aunt. He has not." But even as she said it she was reminded that she had no idea how Barty had spent the time that they had been away.

She met Barty on the upstairs landing. "Where have you been?" she said. But, as she spoke, she was already

66

on her knees picking the straw off his clothes. She knew perfectly well.

"The barn."

"Is it alive?" She looked up fearfully at him.

"Stone dead," said Barty as if he did not care.

Laura ran into her room. Shutting the door and leaning against it, she cried into the fold of her cloak.

Barty heard her crying on the landing. He felt contrite then and going to the door called softly through, "I saw that boy again."

The crying hushed. He heard the door-handle rattle. Laura came out again, staring at him. "What did he do?"

"I told him it was my barn. I told him to get the hell out of it."

"Barty!" She clapped her hand over his mouth, but he twisted free.

"We had a fight," he said. "I licked him. I could lick him any day."

CHAPTER SIX

As soon as Barty had been released from the dinner-table he had run out of the house and headed for the barn. He ran with his mind wholly taken up with the surface of the ground. The scuffed toes of his boots appeared at the edges of his vision, guided past mud and water, aimed at the hollows by the tufts of faded grass. To one side of him, blurred it seemed by their own motion, were the live fluid trees with their tangle of black and brilliant green, reaching out in places so that he must swerve to avoid them. To the other side the rough skin of the wall glided past him. For the moment he did not think at all of what lay on the other side of it. He was going to see the calf.

His uneasiness about those other children was almost entirely banished by the sunlight. They were twilight creatures, scarcely real. To himself he called them his enemies. He thought almost with disappointment, so safe did he feel: My enemy won't be there. He won't come till the trough's full. He's a pig. He laughed aloud. He meant the bigger boy. He did not care about the others.

He slowed his run and looked about him. There was no one in sight. He leant down and put two or three little apples in his jacket pocket, for shot in case he came.

Barty was almost at the barn door when he saw that the cow had wandered out into the muddy yard and was dragging hay from a manger. He leant against the barn wall in the cold winter sunlight, watching her, breathing in the hay smell and dung smell. His attention was completely taken up with the cow and the absorption with which the cow was eating. She strained her head forward to the food and rolled her eyes as if she swam against a torrent. He watched her curl her tongue around the hay and then toss it into the air. She played with it as she ate it. The hay whispered. Her eating made a liquid sound. *Cow, cow, cow*, thought Barty. In and out he breathed the thick cow smell. He seemed to feel the dry stalks fold and rasp inside his own throat. How could she eat it?

The calf was not with her. He had noticed that at once. He was reluctant to go looking for it but that was why he had come. He pulled the barn door as far back into the mud as he could before he looked around it into the barn. He saw the calf right away, lying alone on its side just beyond the long quivering ramp of sunlight the door had admitted. A great silence seemed to crowd about it, filling all the spaces of the barn. Dust raced and sparkled in the sun. It might be sleeping, Barty thought. He went no further but stayed staring at the calf's brown flank until he fancied he saw it move. It might be alive. Nothing could live in such a silence. He went a few paces closer, crossing the panel of sunlight. A voice said, "Who are you?"

Barty's whole body was jerked and shaken. He had been thinking only of the calf. Now this voice came from somewhere else. He turned around. His heart was beating very fast. The sun dazzled his eyes. The rest of the barn was lost in darkness. He stepped quickly back into the shadows, looking around him, panting. It is my enemy, he thought.

His hand tightened on one of the apples in his pocket. He felt it yield stickily under his fingers. What sort of a weapon was that? What was the good of it? Only good for scaring beggars. For now his very same enemy was powerful and out of sight, able to wait, watching, as Barty had been then. He knew, all along his skin, that next his enemy would jump out at him, but from what direction? "I didn't run away from him," he told himself as if he were telling it to some other fellow afterwards. "He ran away. I didn't." The straw rustled by the high stack. He was sliding down. There was the slight thud of his landing. Then the sound of the straw again. He was walking forward, a boy with his hands in his pockets and a close-cropped head. The same boy, Barty was sure, but by his face he would never have known him. Barty stood where he was, weighing his heels against the floorboards, wanting to run.

The boy came slowly forward saying in the same bullying tone, "Who are you then?"

Barty heard his own voice. It seemed above his head somewhere, shrill and feeble. "You get out of here. It's

70

my barn. You don't belong here."

"The hell it is," said the boy.

"It's my barn." He sounded better that time.

"The hell it is," said the boy again. He came closer, crouching a little, moving from side to side: a face like a white wedge, sharp at the chin. "You watch it, see? It's my place. You just watch it. There's not enough to go around." He spoke with a desperate determination that drove Barty back before him.

He's older than me, thought Barty. Quite a bit older. He could see the skin under the boy's eyes was puffy like an old person's, and under the puffy part were dark lines as if someone with dirty fingers had dragged them down his cheeks.

The boy advanced; Barty shuffled back towards the door with very small steps. They were staring at each other all the time. Barty backed into the shaft of sunlight and felt it warm between his shoulders. It made him feel better. He stood his ground again. The boy was no taller than he. He was very thin.

"I bet he's a coward!" he said to himself, but again as if he were telling some other fellow. "I bet I could beat him any day." His heart beat so loud his whole body seemed to vibrate. His breath was thick in his mouth and tasted of buttermilk.

But the boy's expression had altered now that he had seen Barty in the sunlight. He seemed to have expected one thing and found another. His eye slid away from Barty's face and travelled down over his clothes and boots. "Here," he said suspiciously. "You're not from Drouet's place then?"

"No," said Barty blankly.

"Was it you last night then?"

"Might have been," said Barty. He felt that he was getting the upper hand.

"You going to tell I took that food?"

Barty hadn't decided yet whether he would or not. He wouldn't tell his uncle but he might tell the cowman in passing if they met. He said, "Why should I?"

"Get me a beating."

"What good would that do me?"

The boy shrugged. "What are you here for then?"

"To see the calf," said Barty. "I told you. It's my barn."

But the boy did not contradict him this time. He looked quickly about the barn. "She birthed then? Where is it?"

"Over there." As soon as Barty had remembered the calf he had begun to whisper. "It looks dead."

The boy whispered too, but scornfully, "Can't you tell?"

They went a few steps towards it and stopped. The calf lay quite still just as it had done. The boy took a stone from his pocket and hurled it at the body in the straw. They heard it strike the flesh and then the floor. There was no movement at all. "It's dead all right," said the boy carelessly. He ran back into the sunlight by the door and turned to face Barty sticking out his thin chest and swaggering. He said in a loud hoarse voice, "You got a penny?"

Barty could feel himself scowling. The skin all over his head seemed to creep with dislike of the boy. The stone he knew had been intended as a weapon against himself. His stomach had lurched when it sounded on that unfeeling flesh. "What did you do that for?" he said angrily.

The boy began to dance about from foot to foot. "Give me a penny and I'll let you take a punch at me. Hard as you like. Come on. Right on the nose if you like. See if I care. But I'll see your penny first."

"No thank you," said Barty. He felt insulted by the request. He said to himself, "What does he think I am?"

"Come on," said the boy in a coaxing voice, poking his face forward. "I shan't say nothing about it. Come on, you're bigger than me. I shan't blub. Shan't make a sound."

"No thank you," said Barty again. He could see the boy's thinness. He's a weed, he thought. Not worth fighting. He eats garbage. His own swelling anger frightened him and made him feel wretched.

"You a coward or something?"

"No," said Barty kicking over the straw savagely. Slow thick anger pressed against the inside of his ribs. "Here, have a penny." *Beggar,* he thought.

The boy immediately left off his fighting stance and went down on one knee. "Toss you for it then."

"What's the point?" said Barty furiously. "If I win all I get is my own penny back."

"If you win," said the boy obligingly, "you can hit me for nothing."

"Shut up," said Barty. "What do you take me for?"

"Give us the penny then and I'll tell you."

Barty took from his pocket the penny his father had

given him for spending money and flung it on the straw. The boy knelt, retrieved it from the straw and was on his feet again all in one movement. He never took his eyes off Barty as if he expected him to cheat over the coin at the last. He put the penny in his pocket and pursed his lips and rubbed his hands together as if that were an end to it.

Barty hated him. He doubled up his fists and began to dance his feet up and down in the straw. He knew nothing about fighting but he knew this was the way you began. "What do you take me for then?"

"What are you on about now?" said the boy, genuinely surprised.

"You called me a coward."

"Well?"

"Say it again and I'll fight you proper."

"You wouldn't stand a chance," said the boy.

"I'm as big as you any day."

"You'd only get bashed and run to your ma and she'd be on to Drouet and get me a beating."

"I'd never. She's not my ma. What do you take me for?"

Without any reply the boy launched himself on Barty. He came so suddenly that Barty in the midst of provoking him was caught completely unawares. The boy's thin legs seemed to twist round his like wire. He felt himself falling and a moment later lay in the straw looking up into the boy's mean intent face and surrounded by the sour smell of his clothes. The wanting to be free of it made Barty gather his wits and his strength. He heaved up his chest and arms. Somehow by doubling up his knees he managed to force that other body off him, grappling with it, forcing it. They rolled this way and that clawing and kicking. Barty fastened his hands onto the boy's arm. He felt his own strength and the thinness of the bone in his grip. They were panting and growling in each other's faces. The boy had his hand in Barty's thick hair and pulled. It hurt surprisingly. There were tears in his eyes. He got his hands on the boy's shoulder and with all his strength flung him away. His knee was in the boy's stomach and he jumped to his feet. The boy lay in the straw rolling his head from side to side. What if I've hurt him? thought Barty.

But the boy got slowly to his feet and stood in front of him, hanging his head a little. "You going to tell we come here then?"

"No," said Barty. They were both panting so hard they could hardly speak.

"God split you in two if you do?"

"That's right." He began to walk away.

The boy called after him, "Here, did it suck off her at all before she died?"

Barty quickened his pace to a trot. "I don't know."

"You tell me when he milks her," called the boy.

"I might do," said Barty over his shoulder. He felt disappointingly little pride in his victory. He thought: I don't care if I never see you again. He still felt hurt by the calf's death.

He went up the orchard kicking a stone and shouting wordlessly, and let himself in through the scullery door. He could see his uncle sitting smoking peacefully by the stove in the kitchen. It occurred to him that perhaps he should say that the calf was dead. Then he saw Amy with her back to him rolling pastry at the table and caution overcame him. He did not want to be washed by her. He decided to go to his room, look at himself in his glass and make what repairs might be necessary before he spoke to anyone. He slipped quietly through the kitchen without either of them noticing. On the upstairs landing he met Laura.

CHAPTER SEVEN

The following day just as the midday meal was cleared away it began to rain. Laura was glad. She had feared all morning that Barty would try to go to the barn again. Indeed Aunt Bolinger forbade both children to go outside, but when Barty elected to stay in the kitchen she made no complaint. She told Laura to bring her sewing to the sitting room.

At first they were alone except for Henry, who sat reading with the rain shaking the window behind his head. The hushed voices his studies required of them forced upon their talk an air of complicity and Aunt Bolinger spoke in a way that was almost friendly, almost seemed to invite Laura's liking in return.

"What did you make of your visit to the vicarage then?"

Laura let the pillowslip rest for a moment on her knees and remembering that pleasant room and the kindness she had met there said eagerly, "Oh, I liked it most particularly." Then seeing something in the set of her aunt's face as she shifted the woollen stitches along her knitting needle, she thought perhaps she should not have spoken so, and bent over her sewing again.

Aunt Bolinger said, "I am surprised. I should have thought there was nothing to amuse a child there except that Miss Armitage is grown quite childish herself."

Laura did not know what to answer. She glanced up and saw that her aunt was holding the needle to the light and rapidly counting the stitches. Her face and voice were distorted with her efforts as she next said, "And what did you think of Miss Margaret Nobody?"

Cousin Henry's head never raised from his book. Laura wondered if indeed he had not heard, or if he merely pretended. She said guardedly, "I thought her very pleasant." Had she by answering at all condemned Miss Roylance to nothingness? Indeed as soon as she had said it, *pleasant* seemed quite the wrong word, altogether too loud and slight. As if she had caught her out in a lie her aunt grunted and said no more.

They sewed in silence while Laura wondered what other subject they might more safely discuss, but as it happened there was no need, for a moment later, despite the discouraging weather, Miss Lawton was shown into the room. She entered almost at a run, with profuse apologies for arriving late or had she perhaps come a little early? Seeing Henry attempt to rise from his book she smiled and waved as if to someone at a great distance, and said to Aunt Bolinger in a particularly penetrating whisper, "I do not wish to disturb him." She took the chair opposite her friend and straightaway opened her workbag. "That petticoat is finished at the last," she said. "I do believe I can contemplate a muffler for the Christmas Tea," and she produced from the bag the early stages of a piece of narrow grey knitting.

Laura had jumped to her feet when Miss Lawton came in, intending at first to remove herself and sit where she had the day before, on the window seat. But she too was shy of disturbing her cousin. Besides, she found that today she wanted to listen to the talk. There were a number of things she wanted to hear, and she knew well that she would learn more with her head bent silently over her sewing than by asking outright. For a question might, as it had yesterday, cause an upset or at best merely provide half-answers and bring the conversation to an end, but it was surprising how much could be learned by listening. She kept therefore to the chair she had been given, sitting close to her aunt, but where she might also watch her Cousin Henry.

His boots showed below the fringe of the plush table-cloth. One big pale hand lay loosely beside the book. The other rested against his cheek. His face wore the remote gentle smile it assumed when his attention was absorbed and elsewhere.

His mother and Miss Lawton both leant their white caps across the bright fire, knitting by feel alone for their eyes never left one another's. They talked without pausing in low interested voices, as if quite unaware that there was anyone else present. Yet it seemed to Laura that every slight movement Henry made, turning and pressing down a page, shifting his feet about, easing his back, disturbed the heavy air of the room and found responses in the little hesitations of Miss Lawton's

79

needles and now and then a quick lift of Aunt Bolinger's head. They were as aware of his presence as Laura was. And is he really listening to them? she wondered. His face and the page of the book showed pale against the dark furniture, but at times it seemed that he had forgotten to turn the page. She wondered if he really read at all and whether her aunt had intended slightly to raise her voice when she remarked, "What a carry on yesterday, Miss Lawton. Did you ever hear the like? Sew for those brats next door indeed! Poor old Miss Armitage seemed quite at a loss. It's that girl been upsetting her. She's no right putting words in the old lady's mouth like that. All that hair. I never could abide her."

Did he hear? Would he mind? He was Miss Roylance's friend. He had smiled and smiled at her when she was not looking. There; he raised his head. He stared fixedly out at the rain as if pretending he had not heard, but he said, "Whom do you mean?"

His mother leant slowly over the arm of the chair to look at him. "You know well enough. That Miss Roylance. She's been on at the old lady about Drouet's place. Has she not, Miss Lawton?"

He did not seem angry but weary, like someone who sees what is to come and can only hope to distract or divert it. "What about Drouet's place? Is something amiss?"

"It's that young madam that's amiss, trying to teach her betters where their duties lie. I felt quite ashamed for her. I did indeed."

"But Mother," he said, shutting the book in exasperation. "What is she supposed to have done?"

Miss Lawton, who all this time had turned her head from one to another, now darted between them. "She was ill-advised enough to bring the matter up when the Ladies' Committee met yesterday. In front of Mrs Rees-Goring herself, she announced that we should sew for Mr Drouet's children as well as for our own. As if our fingers were not worn to the bone as it is, and scarce a moment to see to our own poor bits and pieces. But she was all for going to Mr Drouet and offering our services. She became quite agitated!"

Aunt Bolinger's most scornful tone took up the tale. "And then I suppose each of us was to befriend a poor little pauper child and find out from it if its breakfast had been sufficient. The impertinence! There's never been a breath of blame about the way Drouet runs the place. And he's been here longer than she has too. He sat upon the vestry two years ago with Mr Bolinger. He must have lived here a year before that to qualify, although I can't say I ever noticed him until he rented Lucas' place next door. I could kill that Lucas. Whatever was he thinking of!"

Miss Lawton said, "What, if I may ask, were Mr Bolinger's impressions of Mr Drouet? They must have known one another, both being vestrymen."

"Well, knew in that limited sense, I daresay. I scarcely suppose Mr Bolinger liked him. A pushing, impertinent sort of fellow, forever trying to get more land or this or that. They say his temper knew no bounds when anyone found fault with him."

"No gentleman," suggested Miss Lawton shrewdly.

"Scarcely," said Aunt Bolinger.

"I have often wondered," said Miss Lawton, "about *Mrs* Drouet. She's never been seen, you know. They say she is an invalid. But Dr Parrot has never been called in to her. If he had I should know directly, for I am in close confidence with Mrs Parrot."

"I only hope she does not recover sufficient strength to call on me," said Aunt Bolinger. "I should hardly care to count her among my acquaintance."

"Yet all in all," interposed Miss Lawton wisely, "one might say he was performing a service."

"It is a pity he chose to perform it here," said her friend. "But there's no helping that now, and the best thing to do is to leave well enough alone."

She poked her head around the chair again and stared at her son. "I'm surprised she's not enlisted you to spy upon poor Mr Drouet. I'm sure she's given the Armitages no peace. It will cost her her job. Mrs Rees-Goring as good as told her so."

"That cannot be," said Henry quickly. "The Armitages are devoted to her."

"That's as may be, but the election of the school-mistress lies with the Ladies' Committee. The Vicar has no say in it. If she continues to pester her betters in this affair I for one shall not be sorry to send her packing. There are penniless girls in plenty who cannot find a position in a private house would willingly take her place."

"No, you don't mean that," said Henry. He ran his hand nervously up and down the seam of his book. "You wouldn't do that."

"I would though. You try me."

The smile was long gone from his face. The big features in the bleak rain light were homely and wretched. That is not really him, thought Laura. She wished he would be more angry and speak out in Miss Roylance's defence but instead he sighed and said in a reasonable, almost humouring voice, "But you were so pleased with her when first she applied for the post. Besides, you know quite well the Armitages have given her the only home she has. And they depend upon her so. It would be cruel to all of them to dismiss her. Especially when she has done no wrong."

Aunt Bolinger said, "Then she should use her head and not meddle in other people's affairs."

Miss Lawton said, "Mrs Rees-Goring seemed most displeased. Do you think she will ask her to the children's tea? It would be of great significance if she did not."

"What's the children's tea?" asked Laura, wanting so much for them to stop. And she succeeded. Aunt Bolinger looked startled at the sound of her voice as if she had quite forgotten that Laura was there. When she spoke it was distractedly, as if at the same time she rehearsed in her mind what had been said, what the child had heard.

"On Christmas day the school children go to the Hall and Mr and Mrs Rees-Goring give them a tea and a gift."

"The clothes we have sewn, Laura," said Miss Lawton sweetly. "The clothes you have helped us to sew. That is what they are for. To give away to our village people at Christmas. It is always a very cheerful occasion."

They set quietly to their work again. When a moment later Cousin Henry got to his feet and went to the door, it was not out of any protest. He moved hesitantly, rather as if he had forgotten something and could not decide whether or not it was worth going all the way upstairs for it. He left the room without a word and shut the door carefully and quietly behind him.

Laura felt disappointed in him. He could at least have shut the door in a cross way, she thought. I should have done. But she did not want to be disappointed in Henry. She could not afford to be. So a moment later she was thinking: He knows it is no use to argue. She could see the truth of that. It would only make things worse. Besides, she thought, catching a single strand of linen on the tip of her needle, maybe he knows more than he says. They never ask him what he thinks. Maybe he's been to that place where the children are and knows all about it. Indeed there seemed no limit to what Cousin Henry might think and might know. She would ask him someday when she found him alone in a room or on a walk. And she sat sewing and happily imagining that conversation and how it would surely put to right the things that had worried her.

Barty stood in the kitchen for a while watching Amy at work. He was in the way. She would not let him help and twice she had asked him if he would stand somewhere else. When Uncle Bolinger came to smoke his afternoon pipe by the stove he felt more in the way than ever.

Beside the stove there was a large dresser that filled

the height of the wall with rows of plates and platters. Underneath were some drawers, and underneath them doors that stood slightly ajar. Barty looked inside and saw cooking and preserving pans neatly stacked in two piles. He found he could just crawl in and sit quite comfortably with his back against the side of the cupboard and one foot wedged between the pans. With his other foot he propped open the cupboard door so that he might see into the kitchen. He liked it there. It was warm and private.

When Amy bent to slide in a pan and saw him, she smiled and said, "Your ma used to play in that same cupboard when she was a little girl—in the old house."

He tried to imagine his mother small, with a child's face, but he could not. He tried to see her face as he had last seen it but it would not come. He managed to reach into his pocket and find his two bones. In the dark he turned them this way and that, trying to fit them together, for they did fit, suddenly and perfectly, if you had them just so. He wondered how many days he had been here. He tried to count back over the meals he had eaten, but almost immediately lost count. He wondered when they would let him go home again.

The kitchen lay still in the lull between clearing away the dinner things and the preparation of the lamps. Fire glowed in the grate, heavy kettles rattled and steamed on the black stove. The clock ticked. Uncle Bolinger sat balanced on a wooden chair that seemed too small to support him. The long white stem of his pipe rested against his corded coat sleeve. From his hiding place Barty watched him scoop the bowl of it into a pile of loose tobacco in his cupped hand and ram it home with his short thick fingers. He was grateful to Amy for not telling his uncle where he was.

From inside the cupboard he heard Henry's voice say, "May I sit here for a while?" He saw Amy slapping at the chair opposite his Uncle Bolinger with the corner of her apron. She wore her cross look. With both of them sitting there she could scarcely move in the room.

Henry took a spill from the jar by the stove and lighting it between the bars of the grate lifted the flame carefully across to the little clay bowl of his father's pipe. His father sucked the flame down into the tobacco and worked noisily with his lips until it was alight, too busy to speak. When Amy had wiped the table and turned away to reach the lamps down from the dresser, Henry said smiling, "You know I do not mind the smell of your pipe at all. I really like it."

"Oh, is that so?" His father broke off his words to suck at the end of his pipe. It gave everything he said an air of great deliberation. "Your mother thinks you do not care for it."

"I know she does," said Henry unhappily.

Mr Bolinger squinted sideways down into the bowl of the pipe, then he lifted his eyes to his son's, somewhat guiltily. "Well, don't tell her. I like to sit here awhile in the afternoons when it's wet and I can't get about, don't I, Amy?"

"You do, sir."

"So don't tell her, there's a good fellow."

Henry nodded and smiled again. "How is business?" he asked.

"Better than it's been these three years past," said his father, puffing sagely at the pipe. "Not that that's much to rejoice over."

"Still, things look better for you?"

"Perhaps, perhaps. We shall see."

For a while Barty listened. It seemed that because he was hidden they by all rights should tell one another secrets which he might overhear to his advantage.

Uncle Bolinger breathed out the smoke in a long slow stream and leaning forward said confidentially to his son, "I may get the contract with him next door. With Drouet," and he jerked his head in the direction of the asylum.

"Is that good?" said Cousin Henry cautiously.

"It is good, boy. If things turn out as I hope it might be very good. He's got near on fifteen hundred mouths to feed over there."

"Not that many, surely!"

"He has, you know," said Uncle Bolinger. "Potatoes and cabbage daily. That's what he wants. It won't make my fortune, but he's a good man to be in with. There's no one else dealing in those quantities around here, I can tell you. He's a good man of business, is Mr Drouet. Too sharp for some maybe, but if I can get the supplies coming through and the price fixed it will make a good bit of difference to us all."

So it was to be boring talk, about money. Barty wondered if it had stopped raining. He was stiff now and wanted to come out. The men's voices went on but he no longer listened. He put away his bones carefully into his pocket and slid himself out onto the floor.

Cousin Henry looked surprised to see him, but did not pause in saying, "Whom did he deal with before, then?"

"With Hutchins over at Mitcham, but there was a set-to over his potatoes. All bad. Black through and through. On the very day the Guardians came to inspect him, too. Drouet don't want to pay a fair price, you see."

"Come away now, Master Barty," said Amy. "The rain's stopped and you're to wrap up well. See, here's Laura all ready to go out."

The barn, thought Barty. I'll go to the barn.

Because it was raining Matron said that they could come into her room. She only said it to some little boys. The big boys had to stay out in the rain. But Will wouldn't get wet. Will would hide in the barn. She said, "Sit there and don't move. Be quiet." He didn't feel like making a noise. He let his feet dangle, and his hands. They ached and smarted in the warmth from the fire. He felt sleepy. There was a clock. Plop, plop, plop, like water in a puddle.

He liked to look at her. She looked pretty in the chair. She was sewing a button on a corduroy jacket. It was Sunday tomorrow. They would give him back the corduroy clothes he had worn on the day they brought him from the workhouse. He could wear them all day. Then he would be warm.

There would be meat for dinner. If there was gristle he hid it under the potato peelings where they could not see it and make him eat it. If the potatoes were black inside you could not eat them. He had tried but he could not keep it in his mouth. He spat it out. The big boys threw the bad potatoes on the table. When the men from the workhouse came, they said, "Who doesn't like the food?" James Welch put his hand up. Lots of big boys put their hands up. Will did. But none of the little boys put their hands up. He didn't. He was too scared. The Master beat James Welch after for doing that. He held him down on the desk and beat him with his fist. Will saw him. The Master put Will's name down for a beating, but they forgot maybe. Nobody beat Will.

He liked to watch the lady sew. It smelt good here. Of coal. The smell the iron made. He remembered that. Her hand went up and down. At home once by the fire, the cat had kittens in a basket. In that room there was a picture of a lady stuck on the wall over the chimney and a picture of a dog. He did not know where that room was now. Maybe even Will did not know the way to get back there. She was a kind lady to let them stay here in the warm. He fell asleep like that.

He woke because someone shook him. He saw her skirt and the fireplace and did not know where he was. He thought he was asleep and dreaming, that his lids were stuck and he was caught in some dream. He tried to open his eyes but they were open. Open and shut again, so that the room went hard and soft and hard and soft. He heard a woman's voice say, "Oh it is a shame to send him out. Look at him. There's nothing to him."

"I daren't keep him in, Mrs Drouet, ma'am. I take a risk having them in in the rain. The Master won't tolerate them in the house after lessons. And the rain's stopped now." He remembered the Matron then. That was her voice. Her room.

The other voice said sadly, "He's one of the worst I've seen. Is there nothing you can do for him?"

"Now don't you fret. They're often stronger than they look, else he wouldn't have lived this long. Stronger than you, dear, I shouldn't wonder."

It pleased him to be the centre of interest. All the other boys had been sent out. He shut his eyes, pretending still to sleep, but he could feel his eyelids beating. "Go on with you," said Matron. "He's awake all the time!"

He went down the stairs and out into the playground to look for Will.

CHAPTER EIGHT

"You're not to go," said Laura. She stuck out her head towards Barty and pushed out her lips to lend urgency to her whispers for they stood just outside the kitchen door and the grown-ups might hear.

"Well I *am* going."

He doesn't pay me heed any more, she thought, for Barty stood squarely in front of her, his hair falling on his face, his hands dug into his pockets, his will defiant against her will. And he would win. Laura was even now covering her retreat, justifying herself that she had not given in too quickly. "She said we weren't to talk to them."

"You told her then," said Barty accusingly.

"No. I didn't."

"If you didn't tell her about them then she can't have done."

"I didn't," hissed Laura indignantly.

"Well then she can't have done."

"She said we were not to speak with children from the asylum."

"We don't know he's from there."

"He is though," said Laura. She knew.

"He never said."

"He must be."

"I'm going," said Barty. He looked about him and reaching into his pocket drew out a hen's egg. "I found three."

"Where?" said Laura a little blankly, not guessing the purpose of the eggs, thinking he had changed the subject, hoping he might even be distracted from going to the barn.

"In the hen-house."

"Well, take them to Amy before they break."

"They're for *them*," he said scornfully, sliding the eggs back into his pocket. A weapon against them more potent than an apple? A gift for them? She was too shocked to wonder.

"You stole them!"

"Well, I took them," he said looking squarely at her. "I left plenty. I'm going," and he turned and began to trot away from her across the yard towards the orchard.

"He stole them," she said, glad for this righteous anger. For a moment she stayed where she was, pressing her shoulders against the kitchen door not wanting to lose touch with it. More terrible than going with him was to watch him go, not caring what he was doing, not caring about her, to see him disappear between the trees and wait alone for him to come back. She began to walk quickly after him thinking: I am doing wrong. On purpose. I don't even want to go. I don't want to see those children ever again. Yet no one had forbidden her to go. Her aunt had asked her if she had already spoken with the children. She had said nothing about never speaking with them. Oh but that was what she had meant. To go was as bad as stealing the eggs and, running now to disobey, Laura felt a resistance and a misery as if she forced her way against a wind although the failing day was merely cold and still.

The chill air closed in behind her, cutting her off from the house. She was panting cold and warm in her mouth. The misery, which surely had been a good thing, began to weaken and fade, and with its fading came a strange feeling of release as if by disobeying she had stepped outside herself and left the meek governed child behind her, while she—if it were she—ran unrestrained through the tangled trees with the wet grass soaking and weighting her skirts. Her feet sounded a rhythm in her head. At home the cook beat on the side of the soup pan with a wooden spoon and chanted to Laura: *If this be I as it surely cannot be, I've a little dog at home and he'll remember me.* That was how it felt. *If this be I as it surely cannot be.*

How odd, she thought. How quickly I change. For now she wanted to be there, wanted to see what those children would be, that the ladies had spoken about as if they could be reached only by the greatest effort across great distances. I'm going to see them, thought Laura. There's nothing difficult about it. Only strange.

What did they say, children like that? She had seen their voices in the playground rise in wisps of smoke. But what words would they say to one another? "Good morning, sir. Good morning, miss," they had chorused in the schoolroom where her father had once taken her. They had said the Lord's Prayer. The words were the same but their voices of course were different. "Good day, sir. Thank you, sir." They had been taught to say that. It was not how they would speak to one another.

The barn rose black ahead of her. She saw the high doors open and Barty standing with his back to her. As she ran up behind him, she saw for an instant the shapes of the three children: the girl, the bigger boy, the little boy. Then they were gone as silently and completely as on that first evening. They ran away because of me, she thought. Oh, come back! But she did not say it. She stood beside Barty watching the dark, listening, making no sound herself.

The barn gave off a sound of its own, just as it did a smell. Some parts of it could be named for pigeons flapping in the rafters, the pigs shouldering against some inner partition, the cow trampling. But around these separate sounds washed another made up of all the infinitesimal things that moved the air and straw, and part of it must be the breathing of those three children.

She heard Barty say in a brave voice, "It's all right, she's only my sister."

No response.

He took an egg from his pocket and holding it out in his hand called softly, "Look. I've brought eggs for you," as if he coaxed some animal from hiding.

Very close to them the straw rustled, and the boy came into the grey light pulling the little boy behind him. Barty held out the egg. The boy said, "How many you got then? Just the one?"

"Three."

"I'll take two. She can fetch her own." He nodded into the dark where the girl still hid somewhere.

He might have said thank you, thought Laura.

The boy knelt in the straw and laid one egg beside him. He took a stone from his pocket and chipped it gently until he made a hole in the top. Then he gave it to the little boy and watched him drink it down. He made a hole in the second egg and sucked that himself. Then he took the shells and buried them carefully in the straw. When he had done he came back to them and, without looking at Laura, said, "Where's she been before then?" He was smaller than Barty and now that he stood forward in the light Laura could see his unhealthy skin and thought: How tired he looks. But her heart could not warm to him. He was too sharp, too watchful. She did not trust him. It made her angry that he did not look at her.

"She was here when you didn't see us," said Barty.

"Your ma know you're here?" the boy said to Laura.

"She's my aunt," said Laura uneasily.

"Where's your ma then? Gone off?"

"No," said Laura.

"Dead?"

"No. We're here on a visit."

There was silence. I've spoken to him, thought Laura. I've disobeyed. But he does not like me. He does not want me to be here. It's all wasted. She said, "Is she your sister?" nodding behind him into the dark barn.

The boy kicked ungraciously at the straw. "No, she just follows us around. A proper misery."

"Perhaps she's listening," said Laura aghast at the pain the other girl must feel.

"You're bloody right she's listening. She never lets us out of her sight."

"That's a lie," said a shrill voice out of the dark. "I come here same reason you do and I've a right. I found it first, didn't I?"

"Yeh," said the boy reasonably to Laura. "She found it first."

"Won't you have your egg?" Laura called softly. "We brought it for you."

There was a commotion in the straw and the girl shuffled into the light. She moved in a surly way with her head poked forward and her shoulders hunched as if she intended to fight the first person that crossed her path. Laura was half afraid as she held out the egg. She expected at the least to have it snatched. Instead the girl said gently, "Thank you very much, miss, that was really kind of you." Then to Laura's amazement she swept a low curtsy in the straw with one foot in a clumsy outsized shoe pointed in front of her and her arms stretched gracefully, the thumbs and forefingers pinched together, the little fingers crooked so that Laura almost saw the wide glistening skirt that was not there. She smiled shyly at Laura and it was disturbing to see for that instant how pretty she was. One must think of her differently after that, take her more into account.

The boy said scornfully, "What you carrying on like that for? She's only his sister."

The girl turned on him as fiercely as before. "I know how to use my manners if I want to."

96

When she had taken the egg, Laura said, "What's your name?"

"Lizzie, miss."

They stood opposite each other, Lizzie hiding the egg in a fold of her dirty pinafore, staring down at her boots in the straw, expecting more to come, and Laura staring at her but too shy to ask the questions she wanted answered: How old are you? Why are you here? Then she noticed that tied around Lizzie's waist was a skipping rope and she said quickly, "Was it you that I saw skipping?"

"Might have been. Yeh. There's no one else that bothers."

"I saw you," said Laura. "Out of the window. Do you like to skip?"

"Yeh," said Lizzie, but she did not sound convinced about it.

"What's your longest?" said Laura. She really wanted to know.

Lizzie shrugged. "I do my five hundred. I don't do no more than that but I don't never do no less."

"Five hundred!" repeated Laura genuinely impressed.

"I don't believe you," said Barty.

She hunched her shoulders at him as she had at the boy and threw out the words as spitefully. "Well it's true. Isn't it?" Then in her other voice she said to Laura, "My father's a performing man, miss. Human pyramid when times are good and he can get the rest of the pyramid together. I'm the sprite on the very top, you know. The making of the act, my pa always says." She swept again the grand curtsy which had seemed so strange at its first appearance. And then as if to explain the emptiness between her hands she said, "I'd a little dress with spangles. My ma sewed it before she died and I wore it for ever such a long time. But then it didn't fit any more. He took it with him when he went."

"Is that true?" said Barty scornfully.

The boy said, "Yeh, it's true and don't we bleeding never hear the last of it."

"Well he's better than your lot, isn't he?"

"What you doing here then?"

"What's that to you?"

"You keep going on how bleeding marvellous he is, that's all."

"So?"

"So what's he ditched you for then?"

"He never," she said savagely, kicking at the straw with her boot. "He couldn't help it."

The boy said slyly, "Perhaps you got too big for sprite. I expect he took the dress to give it to someone who could fit into it and be sprite instead."

"It weren't that!" Oh, but it was. She had rounded on him too quickly for Laura not to know it was. "He needed me. He's coming back for me. He said I was the making of the act. In the summer when he has a new act. You'll see," she said to Will.

Laura hurt for her. All she could think to say was, "I never skipped more than eighty-four." But it was not enough. Lizzie turned and shuffled away into the dark behind the straw. In silence the other children listened. She had not, Laura knew, gone out of the barn, but hid somewhere listening to them, perhaps eating her egg.

The boy said to Laura, "Is he really your brother?"

"Yes."

"Cor I pity you then."

"Shut up," said Barty.

"Pity you then," said the little boy and stuck out his tongue. He'd not spoken before nor had Laura really looked at him. He was not looking at her at all. He stood holding the bigger boy's hand, looking fixedly up into his face, listening to his words and the tone of his voice with a concentrated love that took Laura's heart from her. He was just a little child; thin, with a large shaven head. His cheeks, which in that poor light she had supposed were rosy, were all ravaged with a rash that had broken in places and left patches on his cheeks raw and weeping. His eyes too were red and sore and all the lashes caked white with the discharge from them. What could be wrong with him? He was a terrible sight and yet she wanted him to turn to her and speak to her. She went down on her knees in the straw, saying to him, "What is your name?"

He hung his head and did not answer, but the older boy bent over him, patting his head and saying, in a sudden, crooning, baby voice, "Come on, then, what's your name? Haven't you got one?"

"Jamie," he said. "My name's Jamie." He looked up and gave Laura a small doubting smile.

"Is he your brother?" she said to Jamie.

"Yeh."

"What's his name?"

"Will. He's Will."

Laura looked hard at the older boy. *There*, she said

99

with her eyes. But he paid no attention to her. He was smiling down at his brother who had spoken up so well for himself.

Laura said, "Did you like your egg?"

He smiled but he looked up at the older boy for what to say. The boy nodded and Jamie said, "Yes."

"Are you still hungry?"

"Yeh," he said readily, for himself this time.

"Would you like me to bring you something else another day?"

"Yeh." He grinned openly at her but immediately turned his face from her up to his brother's, and Laura following his eyes found that the boy called Will was staring at her without enquiry or suspicion but with a look of fixed hopelessness that she could not comprehend at all. It made her get to her feet and back away from them and say stiffly, "We must go now."

No one else said anything. "Goodbye," she called into the dark to Lizzie. There was no answer. She turned and walked out of the barn. She heard Barty behind her. Then he ran past her without speaking.

What am I going to do? thought Laura. She walked slowly back towards the house. Barty was far ahead. She had promised to help, but she did not know how to. If I were home, she thought, I should know what to do. I should tell Papa.

She was standing still now among the trees. In imagination she knocked at the door of her father's study.

"Come in." That was how he said it: a long "come," a quick upward "in."

100

There was a circle of steady lamplight on the desk. Papa's dark head and shoulders hung above it. The little room was embraced by his shadow on the walls and on the ceiling. He did not stop writing, quicker and quicker, on and on, until his cuff rasped across the inkwell, and then again, quickly on and on.

"Well, Laura?"

"Papa, I saw some poor children today."

"My kind girl, did you pity them?"

"Yes, Papa. They were so very hungry. The girl's father had just left her, and the little boy had a rash all over his face. He cannot be well cared for."

"And you would have me put it all right?" How sadly and kindly he spoke. She was comforted already.

He swung his chair around from his desk and held out his arm for her. She went and leaned back against him in perfect safety. She felt the firelight on her cheek. The smell of tobacco smoke and wood smoke clung in his clothes.

"Even if it meant your having less for your own supper?"

"Oh, willingly, Papa."

"Then I shall see to it."

A man's voice said, "Good evening, miss," and in confusion Laura saw the cowman almost in front of her, swinging his bucket, on the way to the barn. "Good evening," she said, and when he passed the vision was gone.

What is it that Papa does? thought Laura, standing shivering in the orchard between the barn and the lighted house. He visited the houses of the poor with baskets of food. He went to places where he would not take her. He kept the addresses and the names of the people in a little leather book. Once a week her mother made soup in the kitchen and weighed it out: so many carrots, so much barley, so much bones, so much meat. The whole house smelt of it, but they never ate it. It went to the poor. Feed the poor. It was an order. Week by week they obeyed it.

Slowly she crossed the yard and let herself into the house through the scullery door. On the shelf above the place where the pig bucket was kept she saw a plate. On it were a few slices of bread and butter and a piece of cake. Laura looked into the kitchen. It was empty. She looked back at the plate. Surely Amy had taken it there to scrape it into the bucket, and being distracted had left it on the shelf. Now if she found it empty she would think that the cowman had taken it. Quickly she took out her clean handkerchief and wrapped the bread and cake in it and hid it under her cloak. It was not really stealing, she told herself. The children would have had it in the end in any case.

CHAPTER NINE

If this be I, thought Laura, *as it surely cannot be.*

A week had passed and it seemed that her entire life had altered. *She* had altered. All day her concern was to find food and take it without being seen. If ever Amy gave her a slice of bread or a cutting of pastry she put it in her apron pocket. Once when everyone had turned from the table to see the new moon, she had had time to hide everything that was on her plate in her handkerchief. That was her food so it was not stealing. Amy had sent her to the apple store and she had hidden three apples under the straw by the hens' nests until evening. Then Amy had said, "Keep one for you and Barty," and she had said, "No thank you," so that cancelled it out in a way and made it really not stealing, all but the one apple.

But it was stealing. Her aunt without a doubt would think it so. She had disobeyed. She had lied. Each morning she stared at the face in the blotched mirror and it stared anxiously back again. But it was the same. The badness did not show.

No one saw her take the food.

No one noticed that it had gone.

No one frowned as she passed, as they would have done at home, and said, "Is there anything *wrong*, Laura?" No one noticed.

Greater even than her fear of being caught was the fear each day that she would find nothing, for now each evening they came to the barn expecting her, watching her silently as she approached, wondering what she brought for them. And when it was produced they ate so quickly and harshly that the food she had worked so hard to bring seemed nothing, never enough. Then in distress she would promise, "I'll bring more tomorrow," and would wake in the morning with a greater sense of guilt and anxiety pressing down on her like a hand.

She wanted it to stop. She wanted a stronger hand to lift it all away. When hooves sounded in the road she ran to the window, thinking each time that it would be her father come to take them home again. But nearly two weeks had passed since they had come and there was no word of their returning home. No one mentioned the cholera. No one mentioned their parents. Only Amy talked about the little girl who had been her mother.

Barty was no use to her, for now each morning he went to Mr Armitage for lessons.

"And who is to pay for that?" Aunt Bolinger had asked when Henry made the suggestion.

"He wants no pay, Mother. He made the offer out of friendship."

"Friendship to whom, pray?"

"Why, to us all."

His mother said scornfully, "I shall be interested to see which of those two contrives to learn anything from the other." Nevertheless she put up no real opposition. To have Barty safely out of the house all morning and at no expense was not an opportunity to pass by.

Laura longed to go with him, but she was not allowed to. She was a girl and must stay at home and help in the house with Amy and Aunt Bolinger.

"So your father is interested in the cholera," said Mr Armitage. He shifted to the very edge of his chair and tilted his frail bony head to one side, watching Barty acutely.

Barty had come each day to the vicarage for a week now, sometimes alone, sometimes, as today, with Cousin Henry. Each time he thought: Today there will surely be a lesson. But they had never yet had the lesson. No books, no slate, no pencil. Each day he sat on the stool in front of Mr Armitage and they talked to each other. When Mr Armitage was tired of talking he leant back in his chair and shut his eyes and that meant there was no more chance of a lesson for that day. Even then Barty would stay until the church clock struck twelve outside the windows. He would walk quietly around the room, staring into all the pictures, smelling the bowls of dried petals that stood on little tables about the room, watching the fire. He liked it here. It rested him.

Even when Cousin Henry brought him, they did not hurry back. Henry was content to wait for him, sitting, as he did now, where the sun lay on the faded carpet like a bright rectangular mat, his chair drawn up to Miss Roylance's, talking to her or reading aloud while she bent her bright head over her knitting and never once looked up at him. He was reading now, in a fine strong voice that Barty had never heard him use at home, but Barty was not interested in what he read. Barty and Mr Armitage were talking about the cholera.

"Of course your father has had the chance to study that disease at first hand, so he must know far more than we who have merely read about it. Tell me, if you can, is he a contagionist or an atmospherist?" He watched over his thin nose amused to see whether the boy had understood him.

Barty said decidedly, "He is evangelical."

The old man threw back his head and laughed aloud. Barty thought: I have made a mistake! His face went hot. He did not know what he had said wrong. He was aware that the reading had stopped and looked furtively to the chair by the window to see if Miss Roylance laughed at him, too. But she was smiling, holding out her arms to him in a gesture of pure pleasure, saying, "Oh, what a good answer! He has caught you out, sir. His father does not dabble in science but believes the cholera to be a visitation sent by God!"

"Well, indeed," said the old man, nursing one knee and resting his chin upon it, "all things are. But *how* in this particular instance is His wrath transmitted? I myself tend to the atmospherists. They believe, you know," he said to Barty, "that noxious gases escape from the sewers and the accumulations of filth in the poorer parts of the city and vanish into the atmosphere.

106

Vanish, but alas do not disperse. There they remain, and this is the part I find appealing, until some electrical force releases them and they are breathed into the lungs of the future sufferers."

"Sir, you will alarm him," said Miss Roylance reproachfully.

"Not at all, not at all. He is interested. Look at his face. Besides it could not happen in such a healthy atmosphere as we are blessed with here. There has been some most interesting work done to support this theory. Two beef steaks were flown by kites — do you fly a kite?" he said to Barty — "over one of the most insalubrious districts of London at the height of a thunder storm."

"What happened?" said Barty.

"One returned to earth quite rotten, riddled with maggots, but the other was unaffected. So I suppose one might say the experiment was inconclusive. I believe they ate the surviving meat and suffered no ill effects. Your father of course would take all necessary precautions and if his theory is the correct one, as it must be, he cannot help but be spared." He rose suddenly to his feet, shaking back his long white hair.

Unmistakably it was time to go. Cousin Henry continued to read but more rapidly as if he knew his time were at an end but would not yet admit it. Only when Miss Roylance laid aside her work and rose too, did he reluctantly close the book, and stand awkwardly, unwilling to pronounce his goodbyes. Instead, after a pause, he said, "Tomorrow it will be Christmas Eve. I hear the holly is very fine on Totterdown. I thought I might walk up there tomorrow afternoon and gather some. Would Miss Roylance care to assist me?"

"Well, Margaret?" Mr Armitage said. "Surely a walk up Totterdown is always a pleasure? Particularly on Christmas Eve."

"If you wish, sir," said Miss Roylance quietly. Barty could not tell whether she wanted to go or not.

"I shall call then soon after dinner."

They said goodbye and walked along a garden path through borders shrunk back to twig hands stuck in the hard soil. They had reached a gate leading to the churchyard when Miss Roylance's voice called behind them, "Mr Bolinger . . ."

Cousin Henry jumped and turned all in one as if something had struck him. He began to run back towards the vicarage where Miss Roylance stood waiting for him wrapped in a shawl. "Mr Bolinger," she said rapidly, "I shall meet you on the green. Mr Armitage sleeps after dinner and any little sound in the house disturbs him. Besides we must pass your way in any case. It will save you."

"But it is no trouble . . ."

"No, no," she said frowning and laughing slightly. "It is best." She turned away, and then called back to them again, "I shall bring a basket and a garden knife."

"I think she does want to come," said Barty.

"Do you really?" said his cousin. He looked very pleased and began to walk quite jauntily in his long black coat and tall black hat so that Barty had to trot to keep up with him.

*

Although Mr Armitage had said nothing about a suspension of lessons for Christmas Eve, Barty did not set out for the vicarage next morning. After breakfast he quietly made himself scarce. He had not announced to Laura his intention of staying home, nor did he mention Cousin Henry's expedition planned for the afternoon, although he had spent some time explaining to her about the steaks and the kites, so Laura was surprised and rather pleased when she entered the sitting room, supposing it to be empty, to find her cousin there with his head bent over a book on the table.

He was so absorbed in his reading that he did not even glance up as she came into the room. Outside, her aunt and Amy clattered and called to one another, but the room seemed locked in an enchantment she was powerless to break. She took out her sewing without a sound and began to work the neat mechanical line of stitches into the linen. She knew that she wanted to tell her cousin about the children in the barn and what she had tried to do for them. She wondered how she could explain.

Perhaps she need not. Perhaps she need only say, "I know about Mr Drouet's children. They are hungry. There is something wrong," and that would be enough. He would bring the food. How quick. How easy to imagine: there, by the kitchen door, Cousin Henry waiting with a basket of food. "This is what they need. This will make them well."

Perhaps he will come with me. Would he? Come through the orchard? Hold her hand? Know just what to say to those children? Just what to do? But first there would be questions. There were always questions. Are you sure? How do you know? Did you speak to those children? Have you told my mother?

It was not just the silence that made it difficult to speak. It was her badness that set up a barrier between them. The shining needle gathered up its next row of stitches. Laura looked swiftly at her cousin's good untroubled face. He would know without a doubt that she had stolen and she had lied. He would think her bad.

And then the chance was lost, for Aunt Bolinger came into the room with her workbag in her hand and some sewing over her arm. Laura saw with apprehension that amongst it was her Sunday dress. Aunt Bolinger smiled but did not speak and began to move with elaborate care about the room, for she stood in awe of her son's reading. Nevertheless Laura saw that his concentration was immediately broken. His eyes continued to read but she was sure that he heard and interpreted each sound that his mother made. Now she tweaked each of the front curtains a little forward so that they could be seen from the road. Now she shook out the cushions. Now she swept the hearth with the little ornamental brush and clattered its handle against the fender. Now she settled to her sewing and began to hum a little rattling tune half under her breath. She had no capacity for silence. It was an offence to her. In a moment she said, "Mr Armitage manages without you this morning?"

"Yes," said Henry reading on.

"It is fortunate that Barty's mornings are occupied or he would never let you read in peace."

110

"No," he said, nodding his head but not looking up. "That's true."

There was a pause before she began once more. "I don't know what your mother was thinking of, letting you come away with your skirts half up your legs! I'm having to let this down before I'll be seen in church with her tomorrow." Apparently she spoke to Laura, but she shook out the poor offending dress in the direction of her son.

"Really." He closed the book quietly and pushed it away from him. Then with a fleeting smile at Laura and as if to move the conversation in a happier direction he added, "What have you to give Barty for Christmas? It is safe to discuss it before Laura. I am sure she can keep a secret." Laura, charmed, forgot at once the smart of the reproach to her mother.

"Only a little thing," said his mother. "I thought that more fitting. There's an old clasp knife of your father's I had Amy polish up and sharpen. It's quite adequate." All the vexation occasioned by the hem was gone from her face. It always pleased her to find a use for unwanted things.

"Yes," said Henry. "He'll like that." His fingers began to stray towards the safe hard outlines of his book. Laura wondered if he would dare to read again.

"You read all day," said his mother. "You'll read again this afternoon as well."

"No. I planned to walk this afternoon. Did I not tell you?"

"No. . . . Well, am I not to know then?"

"I promised Mr Armitage I would gather some holly

off Totterdown for the church."

She considered him acutely before she said, "The children will like that. You had planned, of course, to take them."

"Yes," he said. "Of course." But Laura knew at once from the way that he said it that he had not. He had forgotten them. But now he would have to take them and that meant an entire afternoon alone with him, in which surely she would find words to make him understand why she had done what she had done.

Footsteps were running in the hall, then the door-handle turned. It was Amy, red in the face with excitement. "Oh, Missus," she said, "there's a hamper come from Miss Lottie. All manner of things that someone has shot, and a pie fit for a king. Oh, come and see, do!"

Laura felt warm tears rise at the back of her eyes. Her mother had warned her to expect nothing — but, after all, they had not forgotten. After all they were — as some hidden portion of Laura's mind feared they were not — still there.

The whole surface of the kitchen table was covered. There were two rabbits stretched prone. Barty, standing beside them, stroked their sunken flanks and looked reluctantly at their dull open eyes. He would not think about eating them. There was a pheasant, too. He slid his finger along its gleaming feathers and felt a pleasing tremor in his mind when at the same time his eye said *metal* and his finger, *soft*.

"May I have all the feathers?" he said to Amy. "And the bones all boiled clean?"

"Go on with you," said Amy, flicking him with her apron. But she wasn't cross. Everyone was pleased.

"What a splendid pie!" said Henry, placing his hands on his mother's shoulders and looking over her head. "And on Christmas Eve," he added.

The pie's steep pastry side rose up from the table. Laura's mother made one each year at Christmas and Laura stood at the table beside her, chopping the meat and chopping the lard. She had to do it all by herself, thought Laura. She hoped she would not cry.

"We'll eat the pie on Boxing Day," said Aunt Bolinger to Amy. "We'll have had enough of cooking by then."

She might say thank you, thought Laura. But her aunt did not. Still, it was clear that the gift was very acceptable and Laura, who was old enough to know that there was ownership in food as in everything else, knew that now it would be pleasanter than if they had come to their aunt's Christmas feast empty-handed. But she could not forget her mother and father. What will they have to eat? she wondered. What will they do without us? At the thought of them sitting alone at a bare table the tears started up and revealed themselves. And then, as if no unhappy thought could be held back, she thought: What about the children in the barn? What Christmas will they have? Tears rolled down her cheeks.

Everyone was very kind. Amy said, "Come look what else I found in the straw. Quick now," she whispered, "or you'll set Barty off too." She put her small strong arm around Laura's shoulder and shook her slightly as older people do, half to comfort, half to break the thread of grief.

Down the side of the hamper, buried in the blood-stained straw, were letters and little parcels for both of them. Laura hugged hers to her; Barty stuffed his in his pocket.

"Come now, Laura," said her aunt, "there's no cause for all this. Whatever would your mother think if she saw you carry on so? Go to your room and wash your face. Your cousin Henry wants to take you out this afternoon, holly-gathering, and you don't want to go out with your eyes red. For," she said to her son, "you never know who you might meet."

And indeed it had been foolish of Laura to worry about Christmas preparations at the asylum. Scarcely three weeks before, Mr Drouet had taken candles to his writing table and set out ink and paper.

The fire crackled pleasantly; Mr Drouet dipped and wrote and sanded and folded and sealed for over an hour, copying each letter diligently from the one before, altering only the name of the workhouse in the address and the names of the children at the end which he checked and rechecked from neatly written entries in a notebook. He had always been punctilious in not confusing the names of the children in these missives for a careless slip would create so bad an impression. Finally he came to the last. To the Holborn Guardians, *he wrote.* 6th December, 1848. I beg to call to your attention the children's Christmas treat. All my parishes have for years allowed me 6d. each. The charge is very small and I trust it will be given. Gamble is better; James

114

Hutchinson and Kennedy are very ill. M. A. Browne has a severe bowel complaint. The others appear doing well. *He had developed a signature in recent years since he had had so much correspondence of an official nature. He wrote it now with pleasure: a firm statement with a suggestion of flourish that he was B. P. Drouet. He shook sand onto this last letter, funnelled the sand neatly back into its container, folded the paper heavily with his fist and sealed it with the thick gold signet ring that had come to seem so apt a portion of his finger, though he had in fact bought it from a pawn shop scarcely a year ago.*

CHAPTER TEN

After dinner they set out for their walk. Laura held Barty's hand as they crossed the road. Cousin Henry carried a basket for the holly. He had given her his arm, which pleased her very much. It showed he thought her grown up. He had done so quite without considering. But immediately she felt anxious. She must not lean too heavily upon his arm or lag behind. She must fit her pace exactly to his. He hurried so that often she had to skip and fit in another step to keep up with him. Her grip tightened on his arm. She bent her head, frowning with concentration over the two pairs of hurrying feet.

When she looked up she saw the small upright figure of the schoolmistress walking in their direction. For an instant she thought it a chance meeting, but when Miss Roylance waved and Cousin Henry abruptly let go her arm and hurried forward she understood the true nature of the afternoon's outing.

Miss Roylance's hand, very small in its black glove, touched Laura shyly on the cheek and Barty on the hair. She seemed very pleased to see them and Laura, remembering how she had liked her, was after all pleased too.

Miss Roylance said, "I have brought a knife and some gardening gloves." She touched these things through the cloth that covered the basket she carried as if to reassure herself that they were still there. After that there seemed nothing more to say.

Now, of course, Cousin Henry offered his arm to Miss Roylance, and they turned back the way they had come. Laura saw that they must turn the corner by Drouet's place to reach the road towards the open hill which rose outside the village. That she supposed was Totterdown where the holly was. She walked slowly behind her cousin and the schoolmistress, wondering why they were so silent. She felt disappointed in both of them. They were meant to enjoy themselves, yet they did not seem to know how to. She wondered if she were expected to say anything or do anything, but their awkwardness infected her and when they continued to walk with bowed heads, not speaking, she lagged behind, lifting the crisp leaves noisily on the black toes of her thin-soled shoes.

Barty, like a dog, alternately went on ahead or fell to the rear. They passed him several times poking intently at the ground with a stick or staring up into the branches of the trees that lined the green. Then, in a few moments, he would trot purposefully past them again in search of something new. He alone seemed entirely happy.

Cousin Henry did not recross the London Road directly but kept to the green until they were past the front of Drouet's house and might turn straight up the lane. As they were passing down the side of the asylum, Laura heard her cousin say in dismay, "I have let you carry your basket all this time. What am I thinking of!"

"But it is empty now. It weighs nothing." She laughed. Nevertheless she paused and gave it to him.

Where they stood there was a gap between the old house and some newer buildings, filled in with iron railings. Miss Roylance moved towards it and placing her hands on the bars peered inside as a child might have done. Laura coming up behind did not want to look. She sensed that her cousin wished them away from there, but there seemed nothing for it but for them to stand beside her, staring into the cheerless playground. It was empty except for a single girl skipping steadily with a rope. Laura shrank back. She did not want to be recognised. She was glad that Barty had not stopped at all but kept trotting along the road ahead of them. At the same time it struck her that with the excitement of coming out for the walk and the arrival of the hamper she had found no food. By the time they returned it would be dark. They would be waiting.

"Why," Miss Roylance was saying softly, "look at that child. She is not nearly warmly enough dressed! No one can know she is out there. Shall I call through to her?"

Cousin Henry did not answer, nor to Laura's relief did Miss Roylance call out. Instead she said impulsively, "Oh, why is that a sad sight?" so that Laura, in spite of herself, must look again. The bleak playground made her shiver. The forlorn figure playing, if that were what she was doing, so intently, so joylessly, in such isolation, was indeed sad. And she had nothing for them. Yet they would go to the barn and wait for her. All the time that she ate her tea she would know that they waited there, hoping she might come.

"Come," said Cousin Henry to Miss Roylance, "there's nothing you can do."

He would have taken her arm again but at that moment she sighed, let go of the bars and walked on, wrapping and hiding her arms in her cloak. She said, "I often notice in the school that all the games the little girls play are sad. They all teach them to be women and expect nothing of life. They work so hard at their obedience. It is scarcely play. And skipping especially. All that labour, all that skill, and yet they never move beyond that selfsame spot. One can only outshine another by enduring longer. They are trained to accept their lot so eagerly. That is what is sad."

Was that really what was sad about Lizzie? It seemed to Laura that other nameless things were much sadder. She wished suddenly that she had waved and called out as one would without thinking to an ordinary friend. She would almost have turned back, but they would have noticed, have asked questions she was not yet ready to answer. So she continued to shuffle close behind her cousin, straining to hear what he bent his head to say to Miss Roylance.

"You must not take it so to heart."

"Oh, but I must." She turned her face so earnestly up to him. "I have had it on my conscience that I have done nothing for those children."

"But what could you possibly do?"

"I don't know. I had hoped that the Ladies' Committee might act in some way but they were disinclined."

Laura glanced quickly at her cousin to see if he would reveal what he knew but he gave no sign. He only repeated as if the problem were decisively solved, "There is nothing you can do."

"I can write," Miss Roylance said as if the idea had that instant come to her. She spoke to the ground again, disjointedly, punctuating each thought with a little sideways nod of the head. She seemed to be resolving it all on the spot. "I shall write a friendly note to Mrs Drouet. Telling her who I am. Saying we must have many experiences and little trials in common. That it would be of great comfort and pleasure to me to meet her and hold some conversation about our similar daily tasks. For I assume she teaches them. Surely she must do. Then I shall call upon her in that hope."

"She will be out when you call," said Henry.

"But she never goes out. She has scarcely ever been seen in the village, nor the master, nor the doctor, nor the chaplain. Is not that in itself a little strange?"

They had passed the wall of the asylum and were walking beside the field behind it, where the sewer debouched. A great shapeless area of black shining slurry spread over the dull broken soil. It gathered in the corner of the field, choking the culvert that led under the road. Even in the cold a sour smell rose off it. Laura was glad to see her cousin turn to cross the road to where a wooded lane that led to Totterdown had its opening.

He was saying, "And if Mrs Drouet is in, what then?"

"I shall observe and listen and ask in such a way that she is not aware of it, until my mind is at rest."

He moved quickly in front of her then, blocking her way into the lane so that she was forced to stop and look at him. "I beg you, Miss Roylance, do not concern yourself in this. You can do no good and you might so easily do yourself harm."

She attended to him quietly, never taking her eyes from his. Laura saw her small hand in its black glove move impulsively towards his arm, but merely hover above it and withdraw. How earnestly she looked at him. "I do not want to go. Believe me, I do not want to go, but — do you not see? — I feel I was removed from their life by so narrow a margin that I am bound to care for them. I cannot look at that child with her skipping rope without imagining how she feels."

"But there is all the difference in the world between that child and you."

"It seems so to you, but it is very little. Believe me, it is very little."

"This is absurd," he said. "This is obstinacy. You are reading your own sensibilities into people quite incapable of feeling them."

"I do not think so."

"What would you have me do then?"

"You, Mr Bolinger?"

"I will do anything, anything you ask. I shall go to Drouet's. I shall ask about the children, observe their condition, so long as you will promise me to do nothing

121

that will jeopardise your position here." His voice had hit upon quite a new tone in speaking to Miss Roylance, low and urgent, so that Laura was suddenly uncomfortable at her closeness to them. She broke out from behind them running noisily through the leaves that were thick under foot again, to where she could see Barty higher up the lane. It was so much nicer here away from the buildings. Now all around her the smell of buried leaves was delicious: sometimes nutty, sometimes as strongly fragrant as flowers.

As she caught up with Barty a sudden wind shook a shower of birch leaves like weightless golden coins into the road. "I shall catch one!" she shouted to him. "I know I shall," and she began to frown up at the brilliant floating leaves as if her life depended on it. She grabbed for one but it drifted past.

"Oh, well done, well done," called Miss Roylance. "You nearly had it." And she too ran up between them, reaching out wildly, laughing like a child.

"It's Laura that will catch one," said Henry, speaking quite normally now. "I put my money on Laura. Only she needs to be twice the size." Without any warning he came up behind Laura, clamped his big hands around her waist and lifted her almost up to the trees.

How bright it was. The yellow leaves and the hard blue sky seemed to clatter together. Laura began to laugh too, feeling his hands hard on her ribs, grabbing at the leaves and catching one and then another. But it was only for a minute. He put her down again and when she looked up to thank him she found he was staring fixedly over her head. She did not need to turn to know that he stared at Miss Roylance, standing in the lane, clapping her hands, her bright hair vivid against the dark bonnet, her face rubbed by the cold air and for that moment alive and unguarded.

"Come," she said the moment she was aware of him, "the sun will go down soon." She reached out her hands to each of the children and they went briskly up the lane together, gripped by her strong little hands, with Cousin Henry swinging the baskets behind them.

Where the lane opened onto the bare rise of the down four or five holly trees were lined against an old wooden fence. Miss Roylance held down the branches that had kept their berries while Cousin Henry cut through them with the knife. Laura followed behind them with the two baskets, tucking the stiff prickly sprays carefully into place when they were handed to her. They did not talk to her at all, but to each other. They had been so silent at first, but now their voices went on and on as if freed of themselves.

"Last summer I dreaded coming home," her cousin was saying as he dragged down a high branch and placed it very carefully in Miss Roylance's hand. "There seemed no hope of any sort of companionship here after Oxford. The place had grown so intolerably small. And then I discovered that you were here, and all this last term the thought of meeting with you again has quite transformed me. It has made the offer of the curacy seem a gift rather than a duty I had little taste for. I cannot tell you how I look forward to co-operating with you in your work in the school and enlisting your help in the parish."

They did not tell Laura to go away, so she supposed she should stay. They talked in front of her as if she did not exist.

"My work in the school?" said Miss Roylance. "Is it any different from that of the lady before me? I often feel I follow her clumsily. She had taught for so many years, and I am just feeling my way."

"You do not know?" he said in disbelief. Then seeing her face turned so openly and seriously towards him, he went on delightedly, "No, you really cannot see it, but everyone else can, that the difference lies in you, that you are a most superior person to find, quite by chance, in a village school."

"Oh, indeed I am not," she said laughing. "It is I who have felt fortunate to have obtained the post. That independence and Mr Armitage's kindness have greatly altered my life."

"All the more reason then," said Henry quickly, "not to let any rash act endanger the good work you are doing here."

The baskets were full now. They were amazed how quickly, though Laura's arms were aching and she was beginning to feel the cold. Cousin Henry told her to leave them by the fence for they must come back that way. Then he took Miss Roylance's arm and led her up the rise to enjoy the view.

Laura moved away from them. She looked around for Barty but he had disappeared. When she had climbed a little way up above the height of the trees she turned and looked down the way that they had come. The village lay far below. She felt freed of its demands and uncertainties, seeing it shrunken and absorbed into the wide peaceful landscape. Beyond it she could see the dark intricately-cut lines of trees, fading one behind the other to end in the smooth blue line of Banstead Down. Between the rows lay gatherings of mist and smoke which caught the wide diagonals of sunlight. The sun shone on the tiles of the village roofs and flashed on window panes. Frail drifts of chimney-smoke rose through the bare branches. Only the smoke and the light moved. It was intensely quiet. One isolated human cry rose up to them, but the distance deprived it of any force or meaning. Who could doubt it was a child at play?

She wanted suddenly to be with Barty. She wanted to hear his voice and see what he was looking at, but on the portion of the hillside she could see, there was no sign at all of Barty, only Miss Roylance and Cousin Henry walking slowly with their heads bent together a little way below her. She began to run towards the crest of the hill, not at first consciously looking for Barty but expecting each moment to see him.

Already the landscape had chilled and altered. The sun had turned an angry orange and sunk to the level of Totterdown. She watched it as she ran, rolling along the crest, burning through the dark fence of trees that lined it. She stopped and fitting her hands to her mouth called Barty's name. Her voice went far into the silent air. No answer.

All at once she was prey to some unreasoning suggestion of fear. Barty could not be lost, but what could have happened to him? The cry that had floated up from quite another direction still stirred in her ear. She tried again to picture Barty during the walk. She saw him staring up into the trees on the green, trotting ahead of them along the desolate stretch of road by the asylum, leaping wildly to snatch at the leaves, but mixed in amongst these pictures were others, of Lizzie in the playground, and the little boy turning up his ravaged face to his brother, as if the fear she felt, like the cry she had heard, were too general and remote to be attached to any one object. She ran towards the failing sun calling Barty's name.

Then suddenly she saw him walking over the hill with a man who seemed by his humped shape to be carrying a sack. The sun behind them reduced them to black shadows. She was only sure of Barty by his small size. The man was quite unknown to her. They stood for a moment. Then the man dropped out of sight on the far side of the hill and Barty without ever seeing her began to run down to join Miss Roylance and Cousin Henry. He ran awkwardly with his arms stretched stiffly in front of him and his hands cupped one over the other.

Laura went slowly down the hill to meet him. "Where have you been?" she said crossly. "Who was that with you?"

"Look what I have," Barty said. "Look what he gave me!" and lifting one hand he revealed the motionless form of a little bird.

Miss Roylance made a noise in her throat and turned away from it. Birds have a particular deadness. "What is it?" said Laura.

"A linnet."

"Where did you find it?"

"That man gave it to me." He looked eagerly back up the hill but the man had gone.

"What an odd thing," said Miss Roylance, and to Henry, a little anxiously, "Who has he been with?"

Henry said, "It was the birdman, wasn't it?"

"Yes. He was trapping birds."

"He's harmless enough," Henry said. "He comes out here most winters, trapping them to sell in London, I suppose. He's a gipsy of some sort. I used to watch him when I was a child."

"Did you?" said Miss Roylance, smiling.

"He let me watch him, too," said Barty. "He waits till they settle to eat the berries in the hedge. Then he flings the net over. Twenty in one pull." His eyes were shining with the excitement of what he had just seen. "All fluttering about. They couldn't get free of the net."

"Weren't you sorry for the birds?" asked Miss Roylance.

"He wasn't trying to kill them. He keeps as many as he can alive. He sells them to people."

"But this one died," said Miss Roylance, peering reluctantly at the linnet.

Barty said knowingly, "If he gets too many in one pull they die. About half die anyway, just from being in cages. He was going to throw the dead ones back under the hedge. But I said I'd have one — for the bones," he added to Laura.

He went ahead of them down the path, at one minute thinking solely of the light and the trees and the next of how he could hasten the decomposition of the linnet. It put no weight on his hands, but the feathers made them warm. It had felt quite cold when the man had given it to him. He doubted if Amy could be persuaded to boil it up. But the birdman had said that if he would put it in a little box of earth and put a maggot in, it would soon be a skeleton. The cowman would know where a maggot was. Then he would hide it and wait. He would have skeletons of a whole linnet, a whole pheasant, and a whole rabbit. He said wistfully to Laura when she caught up with him, "What do you suppose they did with the calf?"

But Laura did not hear. She had lagged behind and was walking by herself, staring down at the village before it was all scratched over by the branches of the trees. She made out the crossroads with its white signpost. There were the roofs and chimneys of her aunt's house. There was the long narrow orchard and the black shapes of the farm buildings and there the long empty space of Drouet's yard. From where she stood the wall between the two was no more than a thick line drawn by a pencil. They would be waiting. There would still be time to go. But she had nothing for them. She would have to say, "I'm sorry. I couldn't find anything." She imagined them looking at her when she said it. And if he were to die, she thought, would it now be my fault? She felt cold and cramped. She had failed to tell Cousin Henry. It had all been different to what she had imagined. She had known what she had meant to say but like some missing line in theatricals, the words to make her say it had not been given to her and now it was too late.

The playground was empty when they passed it. At Drouet's corner they said goodbye to Miss Roylance. Cousin Henry was to see her back to the vicarage. And then at the very last there came a kind of reprieve, for Miss Roylance said suddenly in dismay, "Oh I quite forgot!" and reaching down carefully through the holly into her basket produced two packages, each wrapped in a cloth. "It was something for you to eat while we walked along, and I forgot it. But perhaps it is as well. It will be easier to eat at home."

"Oh, thank you!" said Laura. It seemed that instantly everything had been put right. She wondered whether the relief in her voice sounded strange, but Miss Roylance only smiled, supposing all children to be hungry all the time. She said, "You will both come to the vicarage tomorrow at tea-time and hear the children sing their carols when they come down from the manor. I know it would make Miss Armitage so happy to have you there."

"Thank you," said Laura again. "We should like to if we may." She looked at her cousin and he nodded and said, "Yes, I'm sure you can come." He took Miss Roylance's arm again and they turned to go towards the vicarage.

"Happy Christmas," she called to them over her shoulder.

"Goodbye," called Laura who found she did not want to think about Christmas although it was so very close·now. She took Barty's hand and ran with him around the corner of the house. There would be time before Cousin Henry returned.

"I'm not going," Barty said handing her his food.

"Why not?"

"I've something else to do."

"Please come." But it was no good. He's stopped caring, she thought. He's gone on to something else. Every minute it grew darker. She couldn't argue. She must go.

When she had gone Barty looked about the sheds that lined the yard at the back of the house until he found a little tin box with a fitting lid. Inside there were a few rusting nails. He emptied these out and going into the orchard, half filled it with earth. Then he laid in the dead linnet and said the Lord's Prayer very quickly. He filled the box with more earth. Then he went to the heap of straw and dung behind the hen-house and dug about with a stick until he found a worm. He poked it down into the earth in his box and fitted on the lid. He watched for a while through the kitchen window. When he saw Amy go through the door into the hall he went into the kitchen and quickly placed the tin behind the pans in the bottom of the kitchen dresser. He chose the corner nearest the stove where it would be warmest, and carefully shut the doors. He told no one he had done this, except, when he saw him next, Mr Armitage, who thought it an excellent idea.

CHAPTER ELEVEN

When Laura came through the barn door alone the children were waiting for her. Now, when he saw her, the little boy ran to her. That pleased her, but today she thought: I might have had nothing. I might not have come at all.

He said, "What you brought today?"

Laura smiled at him. "Are you hungry?"

"Yeh."

She sat down on the straw a little way from them and taking the parcels from under her cloak spread them, revealing two oranges and two pieces of cake, an offering. They all three came very close to her. "Is it just for him?" said Lizzie.

"Yeh," said Jamie. "You keep away. She's my young lady."

His brother said, "You have a whole bit, Jamie, then you share the rest. Be a good boy now."

"Yeh, Will." He squatted down in the straw and crammed one piece of cake into his mouth with his dirty hands. The other he broke gravely into two and

131

handed up to his brother and Lizzie. They ate rapidly, first the cake and then the oranges. Will carefully went over his hands with his tongue when he was finished.

"Thank you, miss," said Lizzie. She took her portion of the food away behind the straw to eat it where Laura could not see her.

"You got any more, miss?"

"That's rude, Jamie," said his brother. "That's bad."

"I'm sorry there's no more," said Laura. "It's hard to take it without their seeing." It weighed upon her that she had brought so little, that the child looked no different. She sat on a pile of straw not wanting to go yet, but not knowing either what she might say to them.

The big boy said to her, "Is he milking the cow regular then?"

"Yes I think so," said Laura. "Did you know the calf had died?"

"It was me that found it."

"I'd hoped it would live," said Laura sadly.

"If it had lived she'd never have let us near her. You see it birthed then?"

"Yes," said Laura, for surely she very nearly had.

"Queer, isn't it. Not nice really. Our old cat eats up the gubbins afterwards. It makes me sick."

She knew he spoke of the part she had not seen, but she said casually, "I didn't mind."

"Ever seen a baby birthed?"

"That's different," said Laura quickly.

"No it's not," said Lizzie's voice from behind the straw. But Will wasn't really interested in that. He was interested in the cow. He said to his brother, "You

132

brave enough to have a suck at the old cow's teats, Jamie?" and he rubbed his hands hard up the back of the little boy's stubble head. "Just like the little calf would have done? You brave enough, Jamie?"

"Yeh," said Jamie, very hoarse. "Yeh, Will, I'm brave enough."

"He is, too," said the other proudly to Laura. "He'll do anything. You just have to tell him and he trots off and does it. He don't look much but he's that brave. But there's one thing he can't abide, see." He had come over and stretched himself out on the straw, propping his sharp chin on his hand, looking up at Laura. Jamie came and sat against him. "You can't abide rats, can you, Jamie. When he hears them at night skittering and bickering in the attics, then he gets in between Derbyshire and me in the bed and shakes all over and wets like as not. That's dirty, isn't it, Jamie?"

"Yeh," said Jamie.

"He won't get out to the bucket if he thinks there's a rat about. Fancy being feared of a little rat and brave enough to go under the hooves of a blasted great cow. Don't make sense, Jamie."

"Rats is vicious," said Jamie looking up at him.

"How do you know? You never met one face to face."

"They tears you to pieces if they gets the chance."

"Give over," said Lizzie scrambling out from her hiding place and coming to sit near them.

"What's wrong with him?" said Laura. The question had tormented her for days. Now it was out. She did not look at either of them as she asked it.

133

"What you mean what's wrong with him?"

"His eyes," said Laura. "And his face." He smelt, too, an unpleasant sickly odour. She thought Will would not answer, but in a moment she heard him speak in the slow sing-song voice he used for his little brother.

"Your eyes are sore, ain't they, Jamie? Been like that since three days after he came. But he don't mind it much, only they feed him in the sickroom away from me so it's hard for me to slip him bits. That's why he's a bit down."

"Is he always hungry?"

"Of course he's hungry," said Will sliding the sleeve up the child's thin arm in which the wrist and elbow bulged. "He's not big enough to stand up for himself, so he don't get enough to eat. There's nothing to him. But he don't complain and not being brought up nice, he'll eat anything. That's why I bring him to the trough. Things I wouldn't put in my mouth, why he'll chew away on quite contented, won't you, Jamie? I'm feeding him up, see, so he'll be some use when we get out of here. He's a good boy really."

"Are your mother and father dead?" She dared to ask because he had asked.

"No," he said scornfully. "Only they're not much use to us now, being in the workhouse. The worst day's work I ever did was staying along with the old man when he cracked up. He was a coster, had his own donkey and barrow and all. But he was sick and trade was bad. He sold the donkey and then he was so sick he couldn't pull the barrow and he wouldn't let me do all the pulling cos he needed me to do the shouting, and my ma was expecting again so he says, 'We'll go to the House just till the winter's over and the baby's born.' I never saw him give in like that before, and I'd have left him then and there and set up on my own and taken the boy with me, and Christ I wish I had for we'd have made do. The boy's sharper than he looks and a devil for the work, aren't you, Jamie? But the old man goes on and on saying the boy's too small to sleep rough and in the end we all goes in together, but it wasn't together at all, for they sent us here where it's just a waste of time."

"What sort of a place is it?" she asked.

A moment ago he had sounded capable of anything. Now she thought, as she had at first, that something had left him very tired. He said, "Why I tell you it's no sort of place at all."

"How long do you have to stay?"

He shrugged. "Till someone comes and takes us away."

"When will that be?"

"Never," said Lizzie.

"But you said they would come. Your father," said Laura, indignant at her disloyalty. "You said you'd be sprite again when summer comes."

"Well he won't. He's no use. He won't come and I don't care about him."

"He will," said Laura shrilly, and then because she could not bear to be denied, added quickly to Will, "Don't they feed you anything in there?"

"Oh," he said, "they feed us, but half of it you can't eat and there's never enough in any case. Look at Jamie.

135

He was a pretty little fellow when we came in. D'ye remember him when we came here, Liz? Did you ever see him when he came?"

"Na," said Lizzie. "He's always looked bad since I knew him."

"He had real pretty curls, didn't you, Jamie? And there weren't a thing wrong with his eyes till he came here and none of us ever had the itch at home. We'd have died of shame sooner. Just look at him, and how's he to get better if nothing ever changes? I do what I can for him, but what's that? Christ, I get hungry often enough. I put a bit by, but often before I see him I eats it myself. I hates myself for it, but I can't help it, can I, Jamie?"

"That's all right, Will."

"Can't you tell anyone?" asked Laura.

"Who'd we tell?"

"Your father?"

"Yeh. I told him when he came to see us once, but what good could he do? Who'd listen to a bust up old pauper? What good did it do?"

"Isn't there *anyone*?" said Laura.

"No," he said. "There isn't anyone but me."

"Why don't you run away?"

"We couldn't make it in the winter. He'd be dead in the month."

"Dead?" repeated Laura stupidly as if it were a word she could not understand. It shocked her that he should say it right out with the little boy looking attentively at him, accepting that he might die because his brother said so.

136

"Yeh. Dead. You just have a feel of him."

She did not want to touch him.

"He used to have quite a bit of weight on him, didn't you, Jamie? When I had to lift you up on the cart." He was pushing the child towards her. "Have a bit of a feel of him, miss."

There was nothing she could do. Jamie's sore unhealthy eyes fixed on hers. He came trustingly up to her, staring at her with his arms limp to his sides. Laura took hold of him by his arms above his elbows and felt through the worn jacket the yielding unsubstantial flesh. She could feel the bone. She knew it was not right.

"But he looks fat. His stomach sticks out." She was seeking comfort, not giving it.

"You lift him, miss."

She put far more effort into it than she need have done. He scarcely weighed a thing, out of all proportion to his size. It made her stomach lurch. She set him down again. The barn felt large and empty all around her. The children were watching her. The little boy stayed standing very close to her, wanting, she knew, to be lifted on to her lap. Not knowing how to ask. She could not. She wished he would go away.

She said again to Will, "Isn't there anyone who could help you?"

He did not even answer.

"I'll help you," said Laura softly. "I'll help you."

"Yes, miss," said Will without looking at her, without any hope at all. "Thank you, miss."

CHAPTER TWELVE

Cousin Henry had said that he would do anything Miss Roylance asked. In Laura's hearing he had given his word. How well the earnest impulsive voice had become him as he spoke. And Miss Roylance was concerned about the children at the asylum. Cousin Henry would surely go now and question Mr Drouet. But this was Christmas Eve. Tomorrow would be Christmas Day and then perhaps another day would pass before he went. That was too long to wait. She knew she must speak to him.

"Is my Cousin Henry in his room?" she asked Amy when she had washed all trace of that child from her hands in the scullery and come into the kitchen. Amy said that she had heard him climb the stairs a few minutes past. Laura would not have dared to have followed him there, but it was her evening task to set the table in the parlour and from there, if she left the door ajar, she would hear him come downstairs and might be able to speak with him before he joined his parents in the sitting room.

She carried the little tray of cutlery into the parlour and began to lay the heavy knives and forks onto the cold white cloth. A moment later she heard his footsteps running down the stairs and reached the hall only in time to see him, still in his overcoat, let himself out the front door. She ran back to the window in the parlour and pressed her forehead against the cold pane of glass. He was nothing but a shadow as he left the lamplight over the door, hurrying for the gate. She could see the dark ends of his scarf pulled out behind him by the wind. He held the brim of his tall black hat. Laura reached back and pulled the curtain behind her the better to see him go. She could just make out in the faint glow of the house fronts and the Castle lamps, his shape turn to the right. She saw him walk rapidly up the road. Then he turned again and walked rapidly up the path to Mr Drouet's front door.

He had gone already, without her saying a word. Laura leant back against the stiff plush curtains that smelt of dust and cigar smoke. Comfort and relief filled and warmed her. He would see. He would know. Because she had no other faces with which to fill out the picture, she imagined him at once with Lizzie and Will and Jamie. She could see him in his tall hat, stooping a little to hear what they had to say, smiling kindly at them as he had at her on the first night that he had sat at his mother's table, while they, knowing that they could trust him, told him everything they had told her. He would take up those things and carry them away. He would know what to do and how to do it. By tomorrow, maybe, things would be put right. She need

139

not find food. She need not go out into the cold and the dark. Not tonight, not tomorrow night, not again. It was over.

When she had finished setting the table she went back to the kitchen and took off her apron. She said to Amy, "Cousin Henry went out."

"Will she want dinner kept then?"

"I'll ask," said Laura.

She let herself quietly into the sitting room where her aunt and uncle sat on either side of the fireplace. "Shall I ask Amy to wait dinner until Cousin Henry comes back?"

"He's not gone anywhere that I've been told," said Aunt Bolinger.

"He has," said Laura. "He's gone out."

"Why should he do that when he's been out half the day already?"

To Laura's surprise her uncle said, "He went for me. On business. Next door." She looked quickly to see what effect the news would have on her aunt.

Aunt Bolinger said, "Well, I daresay he'll be back from next door a sight prompter than you would, Mr Bolinger. Tell Amy to wait." And from the way she spoke and the direction in which she jerked her chin, Laura realised that she meant next door at the Castle. Next door at the asylum had never entered her head.

Uncle Bolinger said nothing.

When Laura had delivered her message to the kitchen, she returned to the sitting room and took up her sewing. A few minutes later Barty came in and lay on the floor by the fire, reading. Uncle Bolinger read his newspaper.

Aunt Bolinger knitted. Perhaps they all listened, even Barty who would be hungry, for the sound of footsteps outside, hurrying against the wind. But Laura cared most and heard them first. He had been gone almost an hour.

"So you've deigned to join us," said his mother as Henry came into the room.

"I'm so sorry. Have I kept you?" Was that to be all? Apparently. His cheeks and nose were reddened with cold, but there was nothing else revealed in his face. His ordinariness shed a kind of chill on Laura. Yet he had gone as he had told Miss Roylance he would. She had seen him go.

At dinner the asylum was not referred to. Once, when Aunt Bolinger's attention was taken with the serving, Laura saw her uncle raise his eyes enquiringly at Henry, and Henry nodded encouragingly back at him, but nothing was said. It surprised Laura that Uncle Bolinger seemed to know what his son had been doing. He was one of the last people she would have told, but it did not really surprise her that they should not care to discuss it in front of Aunt Bolinger. Still the warm certainty she had felt on seeing Henry enter the asylum gates had weakened. Tomorrow, surely, something would be said. Tomorrow she would know.

CHAPTER THIRTEEN

On Christmas morning the church bells rang and on the instant it seemed that every household emptied its occupants into the road. The village moved in procession to the church door. The Bolingers stopped by Miss Lawton's gate to add her to their party.

Laura had told herself that she would pretend it was not Christmas at all, just an ordinary day of which she would ask nothing. Of course it was impossible. The very air of that day is different, made vibrant with the haste and excitement of all that breathe it in. Laura walked to church, clinging to Barty's hand. Aunt Bolinger's gift of a reticule dangled from her wrist and in it she had placed the needlecase her mother had worked for her and sent in the hamper. It held real little scissors and a silver thimble that had belonged to Papa's mother.

The ground had frozen hard in the night. All the hurrying footsteps whispered excitedly against it. The bell cut sharply into the cold blue air. The voices had a clarity and a gaiety that could not be ignored. The warm swelling involuntary happiness seemed to carry her away from this place, as if all Christmases took place on some remote and common ground. She thought of the children: Perhaps they are happy too. Perhaps for today it is all quite different for everyone. Perhaps today he will give them enough to eat.

At that moment Miss Lawton's voice, as if it came from inside her own head, said, "Look, Laura, there are Mr Drouet's children come to church on Christmas, and there is Mr Drouet himself."

And Laura, looking, saw a row of children, twenty or so, lined up in the cold, waiting for the villagers to enter their church: bonnets and cloaks and corduroy caps and suits, well-grown, well-dressed, well-ordered children. They were all total strangers to her. And there, striding briskly to and fro in front of them, was a handsome stocky man with healthy cheeks and thick black curling hair that showed when he lifted his hat to the Bolingers. Laura saw her aunt bow coldly, but her uncle lifted his hat and even called out, "A merry Christmas to you, sir!"

But it is not like that! thought Laura, and then her eyes told her: Some of it must be like that. And seeing the villagers pass and look at the children, so well-dressed, so modestly behaved, directing towards them brief seasonable smiles, she was tempted to see what they saw and take their comfort to her, and think again: Maybe Christmas is different. Maybe they have enough.

At the church gate they must wait while the squire's carriage drew up and the family dismounted: Mr and Mrs Rees-Goring, a married son and his wife, an aunt, a niece. Everything about them was very fine, the wide silk dresses, the graceful pointed shawls, their faces so finely carved it seemed from a denser clearer substance than ordinary flesh. Mrs Rees-Goring's descent from the carriage, her progress to the church door on the arm of her husband, all seemed of immense significance.

The villagers closed in behind the manor party and together they passed from the bright outdoor cold to the paler danker cold of the church. Laura sat upright in her aunt's box pew. Overhead in one of the galleries Miss Roylance played the harmonium. The air was sweet with fir and candles. She could hear at last the asylum children clattering up to the gallery allotted to them. She sat with her hand in the little reticule, fingering the needlecase, not knowing whether she were happy or sad.

At the very start of the last hymn Mr Armitage slowly mounted to the pulpit and stood with his hands crossed on his breast, his thumbs hooked into the facings of his black gown, looking peacefully down at the pale discs of faces turned up to him out of the dark pews and from the benches set against the walls, and, lining the sides of the gallery, the faces of children.

Seeing his shrunken form framed in greenery, his wandering eyes almost too untroubled, some of his parishioners feared the final proof of his decay might confront them on this of all mornings. But when the hymn was over, he looked about him, smiled with great sweetness, and began to speak.

"My friends," he began. "My dear, dear friends, we are gathered together on this Christmas morning to celebrate the birth of a child — a child so very little that

He was born to us in the night and is as yet entirely innocent of this world and the eternity beyond it.

"For us to comprehend this mystery and to worship Him as we ought, requires our utmost faith and simplicity. We should believe as a child believes, and wonder as a child wonders. And so, at this season, we are wise to seek out the company of little children, to awaken in them the miracle of their delight by our gifts and our playing. To become as they. To be born again as little children ourselves and so be ready to enter the kingdom of heaven.

"But let us today, as we look down into those joyful faces, see, at their shoulders, other forms: the multitude of children in this land who will pass today cold and hungry, without human love and, infinitely worse, without any knowledge of the love their Saviour so patiently extends to them.

"There are some among us less fortunate than ourselves. There are many in this land less fortunate than they. But to those to whom the hand of your friendship and charity may not reach, reach out in prayer. For this, above all others, is the festival of our common humanity. All children are our own. Let us love them all."

He turned abruptly and left the pulpit.

"Is that all?" whispered Miss Lawton to her friend. "He is so very brief. I had scarce got myself settled or begun to listen when all was over. They say the preacher at Merton went to the pulpit last Sunday evening without so much as an idea for a text, and was inspired and spoke for three hours without pausing."

145

"We were at least spared that," said Aunt Bolinger, and sank to her knees.

But Laura, sitting stiffly beside her, had listened to every word as she had never listened before. She never doubted that Mr Armitage spoke directly to her out of some personal knowledge as to what was going on in her own mind. She never questioned how he might know. Whatever the outcome of Cousin Henry's visit to the asylum there was one more thing that she would do.

Platters of gingerbread stood on the kitchen table at the vicarage and the big black kettles rattled on the stove waiting for tea to be made. The cook bent to prod the potatoes baking in the oven. Miss Armitage's chair had been moved in from the drawing room and she sat in it in her grey silk dress eagerly listening for the sound of the village children coming down the dark lane from the manor. Laura and Barty stood on either side of her and said in the same moment, "There they are!"

"I cannot hear them."

The vicar went to the kitchen door and opened it. They heard more clearly then the thin uneven voices on the stream of cold air:

> God bless the master of this house
> And the mistress too
> And all the little children
> That round the table go,
> With their pockets full of money
> And their cellars full of beer,
> And God send you a happy New Year.

"Oh I like that one," said Mr Armitage. "They always

sing that one." In another minute the kitchen would be filled with children, smelling of the cold, shrill with excitement.

When the mugs of tea had been poured out and nearly all distributed, Laura felt a tug at her pinafore and glancing down saw a little fair-haired girl looking anxiously up at her. "Please, miss," said the child, "I want to speak with schoolmistress."

"But she is just here," said Laura turning to where Miss Roylance had surely been only minutes before, but she was not there now nor anywhere else in the room. "Can I help you?"

"I must speak to schoolmistress particular."

Laura took the child's hand and led her into the hall. It struck cold after the warm crowded kitchen. The only light came from two candles set in brackets beside a looking-glass. Laura called Miss Roylance's name softly once, but when no answer came, more loudly. A moment later the door from the sitting room opened and Miss Roylance hurried out, saying, "Did you call me?" but scarcely looking at them. She went instead to the looking-glass and peered at her face reflected there in the candlelight. She slid her hands quickly over her cheeks and hair and began automatically to twist up the small escaped curls at the base of her neck and pin them into place. From the kitchen the thin uncertain voices of the children and Mr Armitage's frail cracked one sang, *I'll give you one-O, Green grow the rushes-O.* Laura, looking through the open door into the sitting room, saw her Cousin Henry standing by the window with his back to the room. The curtains were pulled back and the glass coldly lit with moonlight. He stared out into the garden without moving.

Laura said, "She wants to ask you something." But the child seemed to have lost her tongue.

Miss Roylance turned and knelt down quickly, laying her hands on the little girl's shoulders and saying, "What is it, Sarah?"

"It's my ma," said the child at last. "Says may she have the little clothes tonight as she thinks she's near her time."

"Oh!" cried Miss Roylance, snatching her hands back and pressing them to her own cheeks. "Mrs Webb! I had completely forgotten. Sarah, I shall air them this instant; there is a fire in Miss Armitage's room. We'll have them ready for you to take home with you." She was on her feet again, and reached out her hand, saying, "Laura will help me."

Laura was pleased to take her hand and run behind her up the stairs. She knew about the little clothes. There was a set at home. They went wherever a new baby was. After a month all the tiny clothes came back and were washed and mended and sent away to another house and another baby. It surprised her that when Miss Roylance lifted down the wicker basket from the wardrobe on the upstairs landing she felt she must explain, "You see there is a little baby coming to live with this poor family and we should not like it to be cold, should we?"

"I know," said Laura. She looked at Miss Roylance steadily. Even *she* made it sound as if the baby would arrive by cart as she and Barty had done.

Still it was a pleasure to stand beside her in Miss Armitage's room, hanging out the tiny garments that might have been dolls' clothes had they not been so plain. Miss Roylance shook each garment, inspected it against the firelight and hung it on the clothes-horse she had set before the fire. The garments had been washed and washed again and often darned, but they were clean and the flannel smelt sweetly as the fire warmed them. Miss Roylance said, "I washed them and put them away after the last time. I had meant to check each one for mending but it quite slipped my mind. Mercifully they seem in good repair." But all the time she spoke in a breathless excited voice as if she hummed some other tune quite wrongly set to these particular words.

When the task was done she began to move towards the window, swaying a little as if at any moment she might round into a dance to that same inner tune. She pushed back the curtain and leant with her forehead hard against the cold glass, smiling into the dark. "Do you see the moon, Laura?"

Laura came and stood beside her, watching the ragged edges of the clouds torn across the face of the moon. If you thought one way it was the clouds that moved. If you thought another it was the moon. It was a wild sight. It made her draw in her breath. Miss Roylance's arm went about her shoulders and drew her closer. Pleased and shy, Laura slipped her arm around the slight stiff waist. Oh, she thought. She likes me. She truly does.

"Do you see the stars?" said the schoolmistress in almost a whisper. "Do you wish on them?"

149

Laura leant her head trustingly against Miss Roylance's neck. "I wish I were at home tonight." It were as
if the words were eased from her and the pain released.

Miss Roylance squeezed her shoulder slightly. "Poor
Laura. It's hard for you. At Christmas, too."

But Laura no longer felt it hard. She leant against
Miss Roylance in quiet contentment. "What would you
wish?"

"Why, you see I have no home but this." She had
spoken in the same hushed vibrant voice since they had
stood in the presence of the moon. "I should wish never
to leave this house again so long as I live." She gave a
pleased laugh and laying her head against Laura's said
out to the darkness, "Is not that a foolish wish?"

But Laura did not think it so. She could not imagine
Miss Roylance in any other place than this, so perfectly
did it suit her. She heard her sigh and felt her arm
slacken and slip from her shoulder as she turned back
into the room and went quickly to the fire. Laura leant
against the curtain and watched her shake and turn the
little clothes and set them back again. "Oh, here's a
hole," she said, "but it's just a little one. It cannot be
helped now. There — we'll leave them airing a moment
longer and then we can pack them up." She began to
hum under her breath the song the children had sung.

Laura knew that in a moment this happiest part of
the day must be over. She did not want to leave this safe
room. She did not want to go downstairs or back in the
dark to her aunt's house, or do the thing she had
resolved to do. She went and settled herself on a long
low stool between the clothes-horse and the fire,

hugging her knees to her, willing the moments to go slowly. The fire pressed warmth all down her side but still through the gaps between the clothes she could see the moon fleeing wildly, but never escaping the dark cold region between the curtains.

She said suddenly, "What do Mr Drouet's children do at Christmas?"

"The good Lord knows," said Miss Roylance, beginning to take up the clothes and fold them over her arm.

"What do you mean?"

"Oh, Laura, it cannot be a very happy time for them, poor souls. It seems cruel that they cannot be with their parents, although I do not suppose they can ever have had Christmas as we know it, and may not feel at all as we do."

"He must do *something* for them," said Laura out of her comfort.

"Oh, indeed he must."

"Some little thing for them to eat?" She was pleading to be allowed to forget them just for a while and Miss Roylance, as if she understood, said, "Oh, yes, I'm sure they had a special dinner today."

"Even the little ones."

"Surely they especially."

But a weary voice in Laura's head said: *Christmas Day and Boxing Day. And who will feed them the next day and the next day?* She said to Miss Roylance, "Do you ever speak to those children?"

Miss Roylance paused in her folding and looked at her. "No, Laura, to my shame I have not. But when Christmas is over I do mean to try to find out more about them. I have hoped for some time that people in the village could be persuaded to befriend them, but people are very reluctant. And really I have no proof that they are not well cared for. They look so well outside the church. Only a feeling."

"Cousin Henry has been there."

For a moment Miss Roylance looked startled. Then she said, "No, Laura. I hope Mr Bolinger wishes to go, but had he done so I'm sure I would know." She added quickly, "Mr Armitage would have mentioned it."

Laura, who knew quite well that he had gone, who had seen him turn out of one gate and into the other, still had no wish to argue. She thought: Now I can tell her, and wrapped her skirts more tightly around her legs, resting her chin on her knees. Her arms, her legs, all of her felt light and relieved. The words *I have spoken with them*, detached themselves from the cramped dark regions where the secret lay, and floated upwards, but she did not speak them. She said instead, "Is it always wrong to lie and steal?"

"Yes dear," said Miss Roylance. Her lips moved as she folded the little nightdresses, *one, two, three.*

Surely she would not say so if she knew, thought Laura, but she *had* said so and now it had become more difficult to tell her. She said again earnestly, as if offering a last chance, "Always? Even if it is in order to do good?"

Miss Roylance laid the pile of clothes back in the basket and folding away the clothes-horse stood looking steadily down at Laura. "Yes, always. How can any good be done by evil means? But you, dear Laura, would never do such things. Why are you troubled by it?"

It was necessary to think of something to say very quickly. "Barty tells lies sometimes just because he doesn't like people to know too well what he is doing."

"He should not do that," said Miss Roylance seriously. "He may mean no harm, but what if he had some misfortune and needed help and no one knew where he was?"

"But," said Laura anxiously starting up from the stool, "somebody would find him and bring him what he needed."

Miss Roylance looked at her uncertainly. There was something she had not understood, but it was her instinct to comfort. She reached out her hand and said cheerfully, "Yes dear, I'm sure they would. Someone always helps. Come now, we must go down."

"And would they be right to help?" Laura persisted.

But Miss Roylance had quite lost the course of child reasoning. She only saw that Laura who had looked so anxious a moment before now looked hopeful and pleading. She said, "Yes. Of course they would be right," and Laura chose to take that as a kind of approval for what she intended to do.

When they had returned to Aunt Bolinger's house, Laura let Henry and Barty go ahead of her into the drawing room. Keeping her cloak on, she went silently down the passage to the kitchen. It was empty, as she had known it would be, for this night Amy was allowed to spend with her sister. She closed the door behind her.

No candle was lit, but the red fitful light of the fire through the bars of the grate guided her to the larder door. She opened it and went inside. The light did not reach there, but she sniffed the rich smells and felt with her hands along the cold crowded shelves until she came to the smooth round outlines of the pie. She lifted it down — it was heavy — and wrapped the edge of her cloak about it. She freed one hand and carefully shut the larder door. Then she moved across to the outer door and slid the bolt and lifted the latch. It surprised her that she performed all these movements with such certainty, as if she had practised them again and again in her mind, for she was not aware of having thought at all what she was doing beyond deciding that the pie must be given to the children. She scarcely thought now.

She moved quietly across the yard but once she was out of the shadow of the house the moon gave light enough for her to run. The frost pricked her face and hurt her throat. It tasted in her mouth. The mud that on other days had grabbed and sucked at her feet was solid with frost. She felt its hard ridges in the instep of her shoe like the rungs of a ladder. Had it felt so to walk on water? *Thou smoothest a way before me*, she thought. Yet how could that be when she had done something wicked? This time there was no way around it. Without question she had stolen. *If this be I as it surely cannot be.*

When she came to the barn door she put all her weight against it and swung it open to its full extent so that the moonlight would reach in as far as the trough. The trough smelt of rotting food. She did not want to

154

put the pie into it, besides what if the cowman should discover it before they did? She took clean hay from the stack and made a nest for it just under the trough on the side furthest from the door. Remembering how carelessly and mechanically the man had emptied the pig-swill she did not think he would find it. With the pigs and the rats it would have to take its chance. That was all she could do.

She closed the barn door behind her and ran back through the orchard under the bitter snapping stars. She went into the privy, which would save her from lying, and sat there for a moment in the dark with her head in her hands. She did not know what might happen to her. She had done a wicked thing. Even if no one ever found her out, God knew. Of course if He were all knowing — and He was — He understood why she had taken the pie. But Laura expected no sympathy on that account. The blurred image she had of God was adult, and adult love, even Papa's, could wear a stern and dictatorial face in matters like this. He had said, "Thou shalt not steal."

"But ... but — listen!" a child might pester at the hem of His shining robe.

"Silence," He would say. "Thou shalt not steal." There would be retribution.

She went back into the house, bolted the kitchen door, hung her cloak and bonnet in the hall and went into the drawing room. No one remarked on her absence. They assumed she had been in the privy all the time and were too polite to comment upon it.

CHAPTER FOURTEEN

While the family sat at breakfast the following morning, Amy came into the parlour and shutting the door behind her stood stiffly against it. She cleared her throat. "If you please, Ma'am, I cannot find the pie." She gave a little rattling laugh at the absurdity of it. Yet she was frightened too. Laura saw her twist her hands inside her apron. She herself bent her head, carefully breaking the papery membrane at the bottom of her empty egg-shell.

"Don't be foolish," said Aunt Bolinger. "It's on the middle shelf to the right. I saw it myself but yesterday."

"I've looked on all the shelves. I can't see hair nor hide of it. I've looked and looked."

"Of course it's there," said Aunt Bolinger. "You can't have looked properly. A pie that size doesn't vanish." She did not deign to hurry her breakfast, but the skin between her eyes had tightened into a frown and as soon as she was finished she went directly to the kitchen.

Laura gathered the little plates into a pile with the

egg-cups on top of them, and carried them slowly after her. Her aunt stood with her back to her, filling the door of the larder. Laura heard her say accusingly, "But it was here. I saw it. There. You must have put it somewhere else."

"I'll swear I didn't, Ma'am."

"Then it's hidden behind something. We simply have failed to see it." She spoke with such conviction that even Laura believed it might appear, would willingly have conceded that she had dreamt it all. But it was not there. When every single item in the larder had at her aunt's order been taken down and laid on the kitchen table they must all accept that the pie was gone.

Aunt Bolinger called Barty to her and taking him suddenly by the collar said harshly, "Had you anything to do with this?"

"No," he said indignantly. He hunched his shoulders and twisted away from her, but he looked squarely at her when he said it. Laura had told him nothing. Still he must guess. She saw him looking at her with his eyes wide with admiration.

"And you, miss," said her aunt. "Have you seen that pie?"

Laura said that she had not. She lowered her eyes and her voice sounded odd to her own ears, but her aunt did not really believe she had done such a thing, although she suspected Barty well enough, and she took no notice. Nevertheless when the kitchen was thoroughly gone over she and Amy went upstairs and searched both the attic bedrooms. They even unlocked and searched the storeroom.

Outside the rain fell heavily, making it a low dark oppressive day with scarcely enough light and air to support life. There was no question of being allowed out. The whole afternoon must be spent sewing and reading in their aunt's drawing room.

Aunt Bolinger sighed and hummed hymn tunes crossly and distractedly under her breath, while her knitting needles, it seemed to Laura, made small repeated stabs at the grey sock. From time to time she set down her work on her knee and said snappishly to her husband, "I can't get over that pie, Mr Bolinger. Nothing has ever gone missing in this house before," as if the pie had performed an act of personal malice against her.

At first Uncle Bolinger lowered the paper he was reading to reply, "Oh, it will turn up," or, "It can't have got far," but in time he sighed and rose and went to smoke his pipe in the kitchen.

Cousin Henry had asked for a fire in his own room and did not appear. It was a relief really. Laura no longer hoped anything of him. It seemed that all day no one had looked at her or spoken to her except to question. It was as if the thing she had done removed her so far from their lives that she had become blurred and indistinct as the grey village seen through the window, veiled in rain. The light of goodness had gone out in her. And already, although they had not noticed it, she moved amongst them like a ghost, unable to draw from them by her presence any warmth or recognition. She felt deadened, unsubstantial, so that what should have been intolerable was not so really, and she

158

wondered if to be wicked among people who loved and understood and forgave might not be more painful. Only at the thought of her father patiently searching out the goodness in what she had done, or the little boy's joy in an endless meal, did her heart turn inside her. For the rest it lay still, a cold heavy thing performing no function.

No afternoon had ever passed so slowly. The very tick of the clock seemed to hesitate as if each minute came reluctantly and faltered before lurching on to the next. Did they find it? Did it taste as she remembered it? Were they happy?

"I'll not rest till I find who took it," said Aunt Bolinger looking straight ahead of her as if Laura did not exist. "And I shall, never fear, if it's the last thing I do, and then I'll give them a piece of my mind they'll not forget in a hurry." She had let her knitting fall on her lap and sat with one elbow propped on the arm of her chair and a thick finger laid straight across her lips, frowning with concentration. The fingers of the other hand drummed on her knee. Laura never doubted that she would do exactly as she said. But perhaps she knew already. Laura found it hard to believe that she had successfully hidden anything from Aunt Bolinger. Perhaps all the searching was a pretence while she watched and waited. Almost, Laura wished the truth were out and over with. But tell her aunt herself, she could not and would not.

Next morning, waking and remembering, hearing the rain still hissing relentlessly on the tiles overhead, it occurred to her that the children, too, might have been kept in, might never have found the pie. She thought: If I were to get up now and run to the barn, it might still be there. She imagined it sitting untouched under the trough. She saw herself hide it under her cloak and run with it back through the orchard, each step undoing what had been done as surely as one might unpick a seam back to the faulty stitch that marred it all. But she made no move, only cramped herself tighter into the patch of warmth she had made in the bed.

After breakfast, in spite of the rain, Barty went to the vicarage. Laura sat for a while on her bed quite still for there was nothing to do. She felt the cold soak slowly into her. She pressed her toes against the soles of her shoes and felt nothing but the slight stinging of cold further up her foot. Perhaps I shall stay here a very long time, she thought. But soon she began to shiver and the moment came when she felt it was unbearable and found herself walking slowly and stiffly downstairs.

She went into the kitchen and leant against the stove watching Amy polish the spoons at the table. "Can I do that?" she asked.

"Not today," said Amy tartly without looking at her. "Another day when I've time to show you how."

"But I know how."

"You know how you do it, but you don't know how I do it," and her lips fitted tightly together. That was all she intended to say. She rubbed crossly at the spoons as if she bore them a grudge. Her face looked altered and stiff and Laura wondered if she might have been crying. She said, "Do you mind if I stay here?"

"You may stay till lunch time if you keep out of the

way, but after that you'd best be scarce. She's coming in to turn out the cupboards."

But an hour after luncheon was over the rain stopped. The sun fell below the clouds and sent a strange green stormy light into the orchard. At the kitchen door Laura and Barty parted without a word, each going a separate way, curious, but respecting each other privacy. The emerald moss on the apple trees glowed. Laura ran between them wanting to escape from the house, wanting to be in the dark hushed barn.

It was earlier than she usually went. "Will he be there?" she asked, speaking aloud to herself as she ran, in a cross anxious voice like an old woman. She imagined the little boy running into the light with his arms held out to her. "I hope he's there," she muttered to herself. "I hope he liked the pie." It was very cold. Colder than it had ever been.

She pulled open the door and stood staring into the dim shapeless piles of straw. She heard the cow shy clumsily away somewhere out of sight in the gloom. She heard her own panting. No one came towards her. She stood, cold and empty, feeling as if some last hope of pardon had been taken from her. She called, "Jamie!" but the name did not seem hers to use. No one came. Her teeth began to chatter in her head, matching the words: *It's all empty. No one's here.* She moved fearfully forwards towards the trough. The cold space ahead of her, the cold space behind, seemed to meet inside her as if she could not exist against it. She knelt down on the straw and began to feel with her stiff cold hands to where she thought she had left the pie. Then she heard Lizzie's voice say faintly, "Is that you, miss?"

Laura was very startled. She sat up on her knees feeling that she had been watched, and resenting Lizzie who gave herself airs and followed the others around.

"Where are you?" she said crossly. "Why didn't you answer?"

"I'm here." The voice had not moved and Laura, peering towards it, saw Lizzie's pale dress crumpled like a sack against the dark straw beyond the trough.

"Why don't you come here?" said Laura. She saw Lizzie move but she did not rise. Laura went and stood over her. "Why don't you get up?" she said.

Lizzie was sitting hunched in the straw. Her eyes looked big and fixed. The skin under them was dark as bruises. "Are you sick?" said Laura.

"I feel queer."

"Have you eaten anything?"

"No, I don't fancy it."

"Get up," said Laura, and reaching down she took her hand and pulled her on to her feet. The dry thin hand she held was cold as stone. It made Laura shiver. She said more kindly, "Are you all right?"

"Yes," said Lizzie. "Yes. I'm all right. Just low."

"You're very cold."

"Yes," she said.

"Hadn't you better go back?"

"Yes, miss." But she made no attempt to move.

"Where's Jamie?" said Laura sharply. "Is he sick too? What's happened to him?"

"I don't know."

"You're sick. You ought to ask to see a doctor."

Lizzie turned around then. She bent towards Laura narrowing her eyes. "Well I'm not sick, see? No bleeding doctor's ever going to get his maulers on to me. They cuts you up and sells off the pieces. All the pieces."

Laura said, "You look sick to me."

"Well I'm not, see? I can't be." She sat down suddenly on the straw and said, "There's times I think my pa's dead and no one thought to come and tell me. For he can't have just forgot about me."

"No," said Laura. "He can't have done. You must go back."

But the bleak voice went on as if she had never spoken. "But how would he ever think to look for me here, so far away from the place he left me? And if I took sick and died, who'd ever think to find him on the road and tell him?"

"You're not going to die," said Laura sensibly. "You must go back now."

She got to her feet then. Laura said, "Did you get the pie?"

"Yes, thank you, miss."

But that was not enough. "Did you like it?"

"Yes. It was lovely." She seemed to be remembering a long way back.

"Did they like it? Did Jamie like it?"

"Yes. It gave him a pain after, but he liked it."

"It was for Christmas," said Laura.

"Yes, miss. It was really good. Thank you, miss."

"Hadn't you better go?" said Laura. "It's very cold." She had begun to shiver herself.

"No. It's warmer here. I'll stay here a little longer. I

163

don't want to go back."

"But you must go back," said Laura. "There's nowhere else for you to go." When Lizzie did not answer her she said, "I must go now."

"Yes. You go."

"Will you be all right?" said Laura uncertainly.

"Yes. You go now."

"I'll come again," said Laura. She was backing away towards the door.

"Yes. You do that."

Outside in the orchard Laura thought: I should have done something. I should have made her go. It occurred to her that she might at least have covered Lizzie with the straw to keep her warm. But then she might have gone to sleep and never left the barn at all. She walked slowly up the orchard, not wanting to reach the house, disliking herself, feeling sad.

CHAPTER FIFTEEN

When Laura came back from the barn she let herself
into the kitchen and keeping her cloak wrapped about
her leant against the bar of the stove to warm herself.
"May I stay here a little?" she said to Amy and listened
anxiously for any warmth in her reply.

"Suit yourself." It was no better.

Should I stay? thought Laura, but she was shivering
and saddened and could not leave it so. Amy chopped at
an onion on the table. From time to time she sniffed
loudly and rubbed her sleeve across her face. Is she
crying, thought Laura, or is it just the onion?

"Can I help?" she asked.

Amy put down the knife with a clatter and said, "I'm
that upset, I don't know what I'm at. I'm going to make
myself a cup of tea and sit down to it." She wiped her
hands in her apron and taking down the tin in which she
kept spent tea-leaves for her own use, put them in a pot.
Laura moved aside so that she might reach the kettle.
She made tea and poured it and sat to drink it in her
own chair without a word.

"Why are you upset?" asked Laura.

Amy tossed her head significantly in the direction of the drawing room.

"What did she say?" asked Laura fearfully.

"It's what she found," said Amy. "A tin box with a rotten bird in it. It was Barty, wasn't it?"

So he too had had a secret, but she knew at once what he had been doing. "He didn't mean any harm by it. It was just for the bones."

"He'll have a fine time explaining her that," said Amy grimly.

"What will she do?"

"Oh, she'll have her say, and beyond that there isn't much she can do."

Laura sat down in the chair her uncle occupied on his visits. "She won't hurt him?"

"She wouldn't dare. Her bark's worse than her bite." Amy began to sup her tea but as she drank she continued to watch Laura shrewdly over the rim of her teacup. After a moment she said, "Well now, Miss Laura, there's something I'm bound to ask you." She had never addressed her so formally before. Laura's lips parted in apprehension. She wished the stern solemn look would lift away. "It is this, Miss Laura. Have you any knowledge of what became of that pie?"

No one had questioned her directly before. She heard her voice, clear and unfaltering, say, "No. No. I haven't." A lie.

"Because if you have," said Amy as if she had not spoken, "it's only right you should come out and say so before more harm comes to innocent people."

"What innocent people?"

"Myself," said Amy with a sniff.

"But you didn't take it."

"Well then, Miss Laura, if I didn't, who did?"

"How should I know?"

"That's for you to say."

"Well I don't know." Another lie. "Indeed I don't." Another. She began to shake in her agitation and put her hands quickly behind her back.

"Because if you did know and didn't tell and as a consequence an old servant and a faithful one as was a good friend to your ma when she was a girl, should lose her good name, I'd think the worse of you for that. Indeed I would, Miss Laura." Her wrinkled lips snapped shut and she held her head up very straight. Then she leant forward towards Laura and added, almost wheedling, "Even if it were to shield someone else. Even if it were Barty."

"But it's not Barty," said Laura, her voice loud with relief. "He doesn't know anything about it." She thought that Amy believed her, but it seemed, too, that her eyes sharpened with suspicion. "I must go," said Laura. "I must go now."

She ran into the passage. She was not running away. She was going to look for Barty to warn him about the bird. Oh, what will she do to him? she thought distractedly. What will she say? But when she reached Barty's room she found he was not there.

Barty had spent much of the afternoon digging on the old midden-heap for another worm. When he managed to steal a look at his linnet that morning he had found its decay disappointingly slow.

He searched until he found a total of three worms. These he put carefully into his pocket. Then he crossed the yard and looked through a crack in the kitchen curtains. It was not empty. Amy and Laura sat opposite one another on the chairs. He waited. He saw Laura run from the room. He watched Amy finish her tea and rise and place the lamps and candlesticks on a tray and carry them into the house. She had not seen him. He let himself into the kitchen, opened the door of the dresser and knelt beside it. He did not hurry. He did not imagine that anyone would be angry at what he was doing; secrecy came naturally to him. It was a means of increasing his pleasure in things. There was no purpose behind it.

Laura, when she failed to find Barty, came slowly down the stairs again. She heard the front door-handle rattle and saw Henry come into the hall. She stood quietly on the stairs watching him take off his coat and hang it on a peg. When Amy came past with her tray of lamps and candles he took one and went into the parlour with it. Laura waited on the stairs while Amy took lights to her aunt and uncle in the sitting room. She watched Amy come out again and return to the kitchen. Then she came slowly down the stairs and knocked on the parlour door. She did not hesitate now or attempt to frame speeches in her head. She felt intensely unhappy and could find no comfort. She had come for help with that.

Cousin Henry was writing a letter by the light of his candle at the table at which they would shortly eat another meal. His head was propped on his free hand. His fingers dug deeply into his hair. As Laura came into the room he suddenly crushed the paper he had been writing on and hurled it at the fireplace. It struck the mantelpiece and fell by the fender. Laura stared at her cousin. The violence of the gesture had been totally unlike him. He was staring angrily at her with his hair awry. He said coldly, "Why did you tell Miss Roylance I had been to the asylum?"

Why should I not? thought Laura in bewilderment. At the look on his face and the tone of his voice she felt as if her skin were withering. She went and sat opposite him, picking miserably at the worn plush cloth. That he should be angry with her over something so inexplicable stunned her, left her feeling cold and stupid. At last she said, "But you did go. You told her you would go and you did go. I saw you." There was the window through which she had watched him.

"Oh yes," he said. "I went." He stood up abruptly and going to the fire kicked the crumpled ball of paper into the flames. He said with his back to her, "It's only made mischief between us. You had no business telling her."

"She said she was going," said Laura dully. "I said there was no need because you had gone already." That was what she had meant.

He said bitterly into the fire, "I didn't go for her. I went about my father's business. I went to sell Drouet potatoes and cabbages, which is how we live. I'd have

169

gone again for her when Christmas was past, but don't you see I'd promised him? I had to go and get that over first, before I stirred up trouble." He had turned to look at Laura now. It seemed that he pleaded with her for her approval. She was surprised he did not know how unfalteringly he had it, even though she did not understand at all.

She said, "What did you see when you were there?"

"See?" He had laid his arm along the mantelshelf and rested his head against it so that his face was hidden from her again. "I saw nothing. Drouet, a room, a fire."

"The children?" said Laura.

"I saw no children. They were in lessons, or at some meal. Yes, there was one, a pretty girl. She let me in."

"What was her name?"

He said in exasperation, "How should I know?"

"What did she look like?"

"She was clean. She was warmly dressed. She was adequately fed. You've seen them outside the church. Everybody's seen them. There's nothing wrong."

"There is," said Laura.

"You've been listening to stories." But something in her voice had made him lift his head to look oddly at her.

"No," said Laura. "I know."

"You know what?"

She could have told him then. She was angry enough, upset enough. The words formed, struggling to be spoken: *I stole the pie. The children are hungry. Lizzie is ill.*

They remained unspoken only because at that

moment they heard Aunt Bolinger's voice shouting in the kitchen. Henry hurried instantly to the door. Laura sat where she was for a moment. Then, taking up the candle, she too went towards the shouting in the kitchen.

When Barty had reached his arm behind the round shapes of the metal pans in the bottom of the dresser he had failed to find the linnet's tin box. He groped beyond the pans right to the corner of the shelf, but his fingers closed on air. Very carefully he had begun to take the pans out of the cupboard so that he might see where it had gone.

His aunt's voice, very close to him, said, "Have you lost something then?"

"Yes," he said without looking up. "My linnet." He pulled a pan out onto the floor and began patting systematically over the boards. "I've lost it," he said distractedly to himself. "Where's it got to?"

"Look at me when I speak to you," said his aunt's voice.

He heard the anger in it this time, but it had no effect on him. "Someone's moved it," he said accusingly. It was he who should be angry. "Where is it?" he said.

"That you will never know. I've thrown it away where you'll never reach it."

"What did you do that for?" said Barty. "I wanted it."

Her face, usually so set, was flushed and shaken with indignation. Her stern mouth tightened and twitched like an old woman's. She leant towards him, saying in a loud harsh voice, "What do you mean by it — putting that dirty thing in my clean cupboard? What do you mean by it — when I have put myself out to look after you! Is that your idea of a thank-you?" She stood over him, threatening him with her size and certainty. "That cupboard has been cleaned out every day for twenty-five years and to find that in it!"

Hot strong rage at what she had done swelled intolerably inside him. His voice was strained and furious. "If you clean it out so often, why didn't you find it sooner?"

She struck him then, three times hard across the face. He scarcely felt the pain, but the blows bewildered him and forced hot tears to spring from his eyes and burn on his smarting cheeks. They fell on her hand before she moved it away and he saw her wipe it violently up and down her skirt. The words seemed forced out of him, lamed and enfeebled by sobs. "You had no right to throw it away. It was mine. He gave it me. I wanted it."

"*No right*." Her words came out controlledly now, infused with a cutting mirthless laughter. "I've no right to throw a stinking sparrow out of my own house because some starveling parson's son living on my charity says I'm not to!"

His whole body shook. He had no control over it. He felt the pain and jarring in his foot where he struck it again and again on the stone floor. He saw through the shaking lens of tears Henry and then Laura come to the door and stand staring at him.

"Stamp your foot, will you?" she jeered. "Do your jig for me. Go on, go on. I like to see spoilt little boys cry."

172

"Oh, Mother, let him be," cried Henry out of pain in himself at the sight of the boy's rage and his mother's mockery.

She straightened herself instantly and her voice returned to normal. "I'm sure I've no wish to continue this performance, but never you cross the threshold of my kitchen again. Do you hear me?"

Laura ran forward still holding her candle and wrapped her arm around her brother. She rubbed her cheek on the hot surface of his hair and glared resentfully over it at her aunt. "It's all right now," she whispered to Barty. "It's all right now." The stiff rim of his ear burned on her cheek. All the way upstairs she went on murmuring fiercely to him, kneading his arm with her hand, trying to comfort him. He kept his shoulders held stiff and tight under her arm. He could not separate himself from his rage and go to her.

When they stood apart on the landing he said between sharply-caught breaths, "I hate her. I want to go home."

"I hate her too." The vehemence in her own voice surprised her. She had not known she felt so, but now she felt free to hate her aunt without compunction. To some extent it was a comfort, a relief, but it could not help her comfort Barty. She must see him close the door and hear him cry in his room alone. And she must do the same. She had meant to tell Cousin Henry. She had meant it all to be over, but it was not. She must cry herself to sleep and wake again tomorrow to find it all still there.

173

CHAPTER SIXTEEN

In the morning, as soon as breakfast was over, Barty left the house and set off for the vicarage. It was a sullen grey morning kept alive by a bitter probing wind. As soon as he had shut the front door behind him he began to run. He ran heavily with his head down letting the stone steps strike his boots. It seemed the feeling might shake loose the weight of misery that had settled upon him; he ran to outstrip it. Looking neither to the right nor the left and coming out into the road he hurled against a man he had not seen at all.

The man let out a cry. For a moment Barty was bewildered. He seemed unable to extricate himself from this other body. His face was pressed against a cord waistcoat that carried a cold faded smell of soap. He felt the man's hands, clasped on his shoulders, tremble, and heard through the waistcoat his rapid shallow panting. A cold frail body; he could not get free of it.

Now the shaking hands held him away. Barty stared up at an old face, withered with cold. Deep black lines sank into the flesh of the cheeks. The mouth was a black hole with no teeth, but the man spoke slowly and kindly as if to a boy he knew.

"Now where would you be running off to?"

"I'm sorry," said Barty. "I didn't see you." He sensed trouble in the old man, as a dog might sense fear, and wanted to be rid of him.

"Didn't you, now?" said the man. His eyes were red and wet with the cold. "Here," he said, "you wouldn't be one of Mr Drouet's boys, would you?"

"No," said Barty. He twisted his shoulders slightly but the trembling grip tightened. "What do you want of me?"

"No," said the old man slowly. "You didn't come out of there, did you?"

"I'm staying next door," said Barty. "Let me go please."

"Not now," said the old man. "If I let you go you'll be off." He stooped so that his painful eyes were on a level with Barty's and there was no avoiding the sour stream of his breath. "You know about Mr Drouet's boys, then?"

Barty nodded.

"Tell me, boy, does he look after them as he ought? I mean you'd have heard something, living so near, a sharp boy like yourself. You'd know if they was harmed in any way. Perhaps you'd see a little child standing watching by those railings there." His purpose, his trouble, seemed to vibrate down through his hands.

"No," said Barty.

"Well, in the road then, and fall to talking and he'd tell you for sure if he were hungry, say?"

"I don't know," said Barty. "We aren't allowed to speak with them."

The heavy trembling hands lifted from his shoulders and the old man said gruffly, "Best not speak to me then," and turned away from him.

The moment his hold loosened, Barty twisted and ducked under his arm and ran off free. His heart pounded heavily. He was convinced that if he were to look back he would find the old man but a few paces behind, pursuing silently. Only at the crossroads, where he turned towards the church, did Barty dare to slow to a walk and glance back.

The old man stood motionless by Drouet's railings. It looked as if he were leaning against them. He had been very tired. That was why he shook. Barty began to run again, not in the steady dog-trot he would have used to get there quickly but in earnest, as if someone were after him.

When he was shown into the drawing room at the vicarage Barty saw that Miss Roylance was sitting on the little stool he usually occupied at Mr Armitage's feet. She sat with her hands clasped about her knees, looking so earnestly up at the vicar that she did not even glance round when Barty came in. She was saying, "It was something Mrs Wren said about the children."

Mr Armitage said, "I shall be with you in a moment, Barty."

Barty found that he was too winded to answer. Each breath seemed drawn across the tight aching passages of his chest and throat. He was glad to be left to himself. He heard Mr Armitage say wearily to Miss Roylance,

"So we are not really talking about Mrs Wren at all."

"No, we are not. We are talking about the children."

"Oh, very well. Is it about the state of being that we call childhood that you wish to speak, or about one particular child?" He poked his head around the wing of the chair again and said to Barty, "I shall be with you directly."

Barty began to move about the room as he was accustomed to do. He went from one picture to another, naming each one with a private name and searching the backgrounds for special things, a bird in a cage, a flower, that only he and the man who painted it might have known were there. Then he smelt one by one the bowls of dried flowers. The misery of outrage against his aunt slowly relaxed in him, as did the panic he had felt when he could not free himself from the old man in the road. He began to listen to the voices in the room: Miss Roylance's rapid and eager, "Do you not want to know what she said?" and the frail precise reply of Mr Armitage, "No, Margaret. I do not."

"Nevertheless I must tell you. She said that news went round the village that the washerwoman that washed for Drouet had left, and that in going to apply for the job for her daughter she met Hannah South who told her that the woman had left because the bedding she was given was so often dirtied by the children that the work was too unpleasant. She was told that the bedding was from the sickroom and that someone must do the job but that this particular week there was less sickness and she would find it less disagreeable. But when she went to the room to which she was sent, the stench was so appalling that she left forthwith."

Barty listened fascinated. He had no idea grown-up people discussed such things. Mr Armitage even seemed amused.

"I should know that anywhere for a story of Mary Wren's: unpleasant particulars hinting of disaster and cluttered with so many 'she's' one ends not knowing which 'she' one is at. Signifying nothing, surely, at the last."

"I am sure she told the truth."

"Some version of it I do not doubt."

"But is it right that children should be sent to such a place?"

Mr Armitage came suddenly alive, sitting forward in his chair gripping his knees with his long bony fingers. "Such a place my dear? Are we not all to blame in our hypocrisies? Such places must be because such children are. Would you have them mingle with the senile and insane in workhouses, or condemn them to the mire they were born to? You do not know, nor would I ever have you know, how they may have lived before they came here. You think that because they are children they are entitled to love and protection, but you, of all people, should know how frail is a child's claim to those necessities whose parents are ill or weak or dead. Who is to love them? They swarm in the cities, unwanted before they are born and unwanted as long as they live. They could haunt our consciences. They could destroy our pleasure in the innocence and prettiness of our own children. But Mr Drouet wants them. I know not what wretched sum per head they are worth to him, but whatever it is, it is enough to persuade him to take them in and hide them from our sight. Is that not what we ask of him, Margaret? Is he not the benefactor of our consciences? Should we not repay him with our thanks? But instead we shun him as we would the rat-catcher, or the wretch who toils in the sewers, the old woman who gathers dog soil in the street."

"But has he no duty towards them to feed and clothe them and educate as he would his own?"

"Have we proof that he does not? Besides, if he did, these children, the offspring of paupers and vagrants, would lead a better life than many a child of deserving parents who toil all day rather than take charity. Where is the justice in that?"

"But Christ did not exact justice, nor did he receive it."

"Ah, my dear," he said sinking back into his chair. "Christ is inescapable. What would you have me do?"

"I do not know, but should not someone enter the institution, make contact with the children, try to ascertain whether or not they are cared for according to the standards of this community? For they *are* children, and therefore they are not deserving or undeserving, or capable or incapable, or settled or vagrant. They did not ask to come into this world, nor to come among us."

"They are the blighted corn that will destroy the wholesome," he said shrilly. "The starveling kine that will devour up the fat."

She chose not to hear him. "Have I your permission at least to try to make contact? Quite openly. I intend to call upon Mrs Drouet."

"You are a grown woman acting in your own right. I believe you are very unwise, but it is your concern." It seemed to him for a moment that her face showed disappointment. What did she want of him? Encouragement? Perhaps she wanted him to forbid her to go. Well, whatever it was, she would not get it from him. She had tired him already. He leant back his head and closed his eyes and heard the soft movement of her dress and her quiet footsteps as she left the room. After a moment he moved forward again and peered around the wing of the chair. "Has she gone?" he said to Barty.

"Yes."

He looked relieved then, but he was still agitated. Barty came and settled himself on the little stool. After a minute or two Mr Armitage took the walking stick that leant against the arm of his chair and placing it between his knees clasped his hands over the knob and rested his chin upon them, so that his eyes were on a level with the boy's. "Well?"

Barty smiled at him and shrugged but he did not speak.

"What have you been doing?"

"Nothing."

"What have you brought to show me?"

Barty reached into his pocket and brought out a tail-feather, that he had plucked from the linnet before putting it into the box. It was all that now remained. He slowly pulled it between his fingers until it was smooth.

"Ah, the linnet," said Mr Armitage. "How is it coming along?"

"She spoilt it all," said Barty. He felt warm tears well

180

up again under his eyelids. "She found it and threw it away."

"Ah," said the vicar. "Yes. That sort of thing often happens. They quite fail to understand what one is aiming at."

"She doesn't really want us there," said Barty. "We're in the way."

"No doubt. No doubt," said Mr Armitage. "I remember your bird-catcher when I was a boy. He was a young man. He'd be old now."

"He's not nearly as old as you," said Barty.

"Ah, probably his son. Of course it wasn't here that I used to watch him. It was in the fields at Pimlico. It's all built over now. No place for birds. That's why you see him all the way out here. They say London will stretch as far as this some day. I don't believe it will, but that's not to say it won't. The birds will lose their liking for it then. There's no telling how far he will have to tramp to find them. What do you think?"

"It would spoil it," said Barty.

The old man edged forward in the chair, watching him intently with a pleased expression. Ideas and the very words he needed had begun to crowd his mind. "We beat the bounds here, you know. We still beat the bounds of the village on Rogation Sunday. It is of some relevance. I don't suppose they do it in your father's parish."

"No," said Barty. He sensed that this at last was a lesson.

"That's just as well for you, you know, for in some parishes it is the custom to knock the boys' heads on all the boundary stones. But in this one they knock the parson's head against the trees, which I daresay accounts for the trouble I sometimes have remembering things. Though of course the purpose of banging the head is to drive into it, generation by generation, the memory of where the boundaries lie. For if ever these were forgotten, our integrity would be lost. As soon as we were so careless as to lose the line of distinction between ourselves and, say, Mitcham, might not the definition of words also suffer? Who is to say we might not lose our clarity of thinking about right and wrong? For it is a very ancient institution: Lupercalia, and Antony blamed for his nakedness, and Caesar tempted with the crown, all of which you will know very well. But the custom was ancient even then, and more intriguing is the element of dragons."

Barty listened, his mind charmed rather than penetrated by what the old man said. He too liked the idea of dragons and would happily have entertained thoughts of them on his own, but he knew that Mr Armitage had not at all forgotten him. He never let the boy's eye go for a minute and would shortly question him.

"Of course," said Mr Armitage, "it has now become a rather jolly occasion, with much recourse to the Castle and the Rising Sun and so forth, but who knows what local saints may once have cleared the spring of dragons, what blood shed, what teeth sown, what may be the composition of this soil which we feed upon and contribute to?" He said sharply to Barty, "Why is the pump by the church, and the corner called Amen corner?"

"I don't know."

"Nor do I, but which came first? The church, or the name, or the living water?"

"The water," said Barty.

"Quite correct. It is the life of the place. The church protects it from the forces of dark. The beating of the bounds evokes Christ's power to keep them at bay. It is too ancient a power to disregard, and who is to say that it has not relevance? For what dragons must we now keep outside our charmed circle? Ask yourself that, and then consider: does not a railway engine resemble to you a dragon? Had you no knowledge of this thing, and heard the roar and metal-rattling vibrate up through some raw new earthwork where the blasted trees still stand and the turf is torn and deserted by all the birds, and then there issues forth a creature black, vomiting smoke and flames — would you not say it was a dragon come to ravish our land?"

"I should know it was not," said Barty, but in his mind he had to fight against Mr Armitage's vision of the dragon. He felt a little afraid.

"And may the steam locomotive be not the least of the dragons that threaten us as London moves closer. Revolution. Disease. Think about that."

The old man had stood up in his excitement and agitation. Now he looked blankly about him as if uncertain where he found himself in thought and place. He said sternly, "You had better learn the psalm, for the time comes round very quickly and I shall need you at my side to remind me of the words."

"What do you mean?"

183

"Why, when we beat the bounds. What else should I mean? I have had the words of the psalm for many years but now I tend to lose them."

"Rogation Sunday is in the spring," said Barty.

"Yes. Of course it is."

"But I shall not be here by then," said Barty. He would like to have known for certain.

"How can that be?" said the vicar. "That you should be sent away again so soon." He sounded bewildered and disappointed.

Barty said, "It's not soon." Then he added, "I could ask my father to bring me back again, for the day."

"Yes, if it comes to that, you could," said Mr Armitage. The force of thought had snapped in him. He sat down again and withdrawing into the recesses of his chair stared at the ceiling.

He's forgotten what he was saying, thought Barty. "I'll learn the psalm," he said.

"What psalm?"

"For the beating of the bounds."

"Yes, you do. It's a capital occasion. You'll enjoy it. I always do."

Barty knew that it was time to go. He said goodbye and went out into the hall. Miss Roylance was standing in the hall, apparently waiting for him with his muffler hanging over her arm. "Will you do me a favour?" she said, stooping down and beginning to wrap the scarf around him.

"Yes," said Barty. He turned so that she might tie it in the back. Then he turned back and looked enquiringly up at her to see what the favour might be. She was holding a letter in her hand.

"Take this, if you will, and put it through the door of the big house next to your aunt's: Mr Drouet's place. Do you know it?"

"I know where it is," said Barty guardedly.

"You may slip it under the door if you like, if you'd rather not ring."

"I don't mind ringing." He tucked it carefully into the pocket of his jacket.

"Good boy," she said hugging him quickly on the shoulders. "If you do ring, you may say it is for Mrs Drouet." It seemed she was almost pushing him to the door. When he was through it she shut it so quickly behind him that the doorknob nudged against his back.

As soon as Barty was outside, the cold got at him and his spirits sank. They could not leave him here all winter. When would they come? He had been here so long already. There was all the time before Christmas, dim space he could scarcely remember, and now it was after Christmas. Each day dragged out an unnatural length. This very day seemed interminable. He walked slowly on, kicking at dried clods of mud, not lifting his head even when he was aware of people passing. Only when he was nearby to his aunt's house did he see that the old man still stood resting against Drouet's railings at the same spot where he had seen him last. Quite forgetting Miss Roylance's letter he turned quickly down the side gate and knocked at the kitchen door. "Can I come through?" he said to Amy.

"Yes, if you're quick. She's upstairs." He ran across the kitchen and stood just beyond the doorway ducking his head to unwind his scarf, watching her under his arm, gauging the degree of forgiveness in her voice.

"You run along and get ready for your dinner. You don't want her to have another go at you. There's been upsets enough."

She was still cross but he did not want to go right away. To delay her he said, "There was an old man standing all morning by Drouet's gate. What did he want?"

"How should I know?" said Amy shortly. "Now, off you go."

CHAPTER SEVENTEEN

It was not until after lunch that Barty remembered the letter. He felt in his pocket and found it safely there. Remembering Miss Roylance's haste in dispatching him, he felt guilty at having forgotten. As soon as he was able he slipped out of the front door and ran to the gate. He looked into the road. The old man was still there, sunk down now so that he sat on the ground with his back against Drouet's low stone wall, his head resting against the railings. Is he ill? thought Barty. He was loath to go past him. The fear nagged at him that the old man might merely be pretending to be ill, the better to lie in wait for him. He walked the short distance without looking at him, quickly and quietly, keeping out of reach of the old man's arm. But the old man never moved.

Once past him Barty ran up Drouet's front path and pulled at the bell. The door opened immediately but only the distance it was allowed by a heavy chain. A young man's face appeared behind the crack. He said suspiciously, "Who are you? What do you want?"

"Letter for Mrs Drouet," said Barty, pushing it

hastily through the gap. He ran down the steps again wondering if he might cross the road and pass the old man on the other side.

When he came to the gate he glanced quickly down at him. The old man was deathly pale. His eyes were shut. His arms trailed on the ground as if they had fallen uncontrollably with the palms lying unnaturally upwards. Could he be dead? thought Barty, awed. But that was not possible. Barty could hear him breathing rapidly and harshly. He went quite close to him. "Are you all right?" The old man gave no sign of having heard him.

Barty ran to the front door of Aunt Bolinger's house and let himself in. He went down the passage to the kitchen and opening the door peered around it. Amy was rolling pastry on the kitchen table. Laura standing beside her swathed in an apron was spooning jam into tarts. "Don't you come a step farther now," said Amy.

"That old man," he said. "He's still there."

"What old man was that?"

"The one outside Drouet's. He's sitting on the ground now."

Amy looked up at him without letting go of her rolling pin. "I expect he's drunk, Master Barty. Did you come close enough to smell it on him?"

"He isn't drunk. He was very clean," he added with sudden loyalty to the old man.

"How long has he been there?"

"Since I went out this morning."

"And it's bitter cold today," said Amy. "I call it wicked."

"What's wicked?"

"Keeping them waiting like that. He'll have come to see his kiddies at Drouet's. Was he workhouse?"

"I don't know."

"Well I don't know what I'm expected to do about it," said Amy crossly. "She's got Miss Armitage and the schoolmistress coming to tea. I've all that to see to." She went on deftly rolling out pastry. Laura spooned the jam mechanically. She looked pale and apathetic. She did not say anything.

After a moment Barty said, "Would you come and look at him? I don't think he's very well."

Amy looked sharply from one side to the other as if she were gathering advice. "Oh, if you insist. Very well then. I suppose it's only Christian charity to take a look at the poor soul." She took her cloak off its peg on the door and looking over Barty's head into the hall, said, "Quick then, you can come through."

"Shall I come?" said Laura.

"You finish those tarts," said Amy shortly.

Amy wrapped herself in her cloak and taking Barty by the hand hurried him along until they stood over the old man. His head had sunk down onto his chest; otherwise he had not moved. Barty could still hear his painful breathing. "Is he sick do you think?" he whispered to Amy.

"Just done in I shouldn't wonder. We can't leave him here like that. He'll die of cold. Come on with you," she said to the old man shaking him roughly by the shoulder. "You're to come away into the warm. Can you get to your feet?"

He looked patiently up at them then with no sign of

recognition. Amy dragged at his arm, nodding to Barty to do the same from his side. "Come quick now," she urged, "before the missus sees us." He began to mumble. "What's he saying?" said Amy crossly. She kept glancing nervously up at the windows of the two high houses.

Between them they managed to get him upright, sliding his back up the railings. Barty slipped his shoulders under the old man's arm. Amy kept her grip on the other. He was not heavy but he had no will to carry himself. He trembled all over now and his teeth rattled in his head. Slowly they coaxed him over the ground between the gates.

Barty could feel a rising terror at being returned to the old man's grasp. What if the limp arm should suddenly tighten about him? Moreover he was infected with Amy's fear of being seen. At any moment he thought to hear a sash thrown open and his aunt's voice shouting. When they reached the shelter of the alley leading to the kitchen door, it seemed an age had passed.

Amy led the man to Uncle Bolinger's chair and settled him into it. As the warmth of the stove reached him he began to shudder more violently. He sat hunched, head bowed, rubbing his folded hands up and down between his knees, breathing oddly. "Warm him some milk," Amy whispered to Laura. "I can't make out if he's sick or just cold. She'll half kill me if she finds him in here! Go stand by the door," she hissed to Barty, "and give us a warning if she comes."

All the time that Laura was filling the pan from the

190

churn with the dipper and watching until the disc of white milk crept with the warmth and frothed at the edges the old man's breathing filled the room as sharp and painful as sawing. He frightened Laura. She thought: He's ill. He's going to die. What do we do with him? She could not keep from her mind that if he died now, where he sat, her aunt would have to be told and that she would be angry. "The milk's scalded," she said to Amy.

Amy cut a thick slice of bread and putting it on a plate and the milk in a bowl set them both on a stool beside the old man. He made no move towards them. "You sit there and keep an eye on him," Amy said to Laura, pushing her towards the other chair. "If I don't get on they'll come and she'll be wanting to know why nothing's ready." She began to take the tea things from the dresser and lay them on the tray, glancing anxiously over her shoulder.

Laura sat down by the fire and stared reluctantly across at the old man. There seemed no harm in staring as he was so little aware of her. He continued to rub his shaking hands looking down at them with a patient mild expression, waiting for them to right themselves. Once he raised his head and gazed about the room where he found himself, without curiosity. His eyes were shallow as if schooled neither to look far in nor far out. She saw as Barty had, the deep lines in his cheeks but it seemed whatever feeling had driven them there had long gone. Much handling had rubbed him as smooth and feature-less as a beach pebble.

Barty's face appeared around the door. "What do I do

191

if she comes?" he whispered.

"Be quiet," she hissed back at him. She had no idea.

Gradually the old man's breathing quietened and deepened. The rattling kettles, the ticking clock, the fluttering candles, reasserted their rapid happier sounds in the room. Amy hurried over to look at him. He straightened himself in the chair. His face seemed to fill out in the warmth. Amy said, as if releasing the words on a long held breath, "However far have you come today?"

"Holborn," he said.

"Walking all the way?"

"How else?" said the old man.

"All that way," said Amy. "I'd an auntie once went away to live in Holborn. She's dead now. Drink up your milk, do, before it's cold."

The old man said, "I'll wash if I may before I eat, missus."

Amy pointed to the scullery door. He got stiffly to his feet and very slowly took off his jacket and rolled up his grey woollen shirt-sleeves. Then he went into the scullery and they heard the pump creak and the water splash. Amy picked up his coat and inspected it. She held it up so that Laura could see a neatly-stitched number on a bit of tape sewed into the back. "Workhouse, didn't I say he was?" she whispered. "They number them like that. They teach them to be clean too." She put it down quickly when they heard him coming back.

He thanked her and nodded to Laura as if he had only just seen her, put on his jacket again and settled down to his food. Laura watched him draw from his pocket a clasp knife. He opened it and cut the bread into little cubes. Then laying the knife on the plate he dipped each morsel in the milk and ate it. Amy and Laura leant against the table side by side staring at him. He ate without embarrassment or pleasure as daintily as a cat. When he had done he drained the bowl, cleaned round it with the last morsel of bread, ate that, carefully wiped the knife on the back of his hand and replaced it inside his clothing. He said, "Thank you kindly. I'm better now."

Amy said quickly, "You're never going back to Holborn tonight. You could sleep in the barn. There's hay there and the cowman would never say."

"I must go tonight. I've a letter to deliver." He spoke obediently like a child who remembers his errand but has forgotten or never understood the purpose of it.

"Who to?" said Amy.

He reached slowly into his jacket again and brought out an envelope frowning at it and weighing it in his hand. "I don't read," he said. "I don't know who it's for. I'm to take it back to the great house at Holborn."

"Ah," said Amy nodding in sympathy to him. "Here, Laura. You have a read of it. You've a little one at Drouet's then?" she said to the man.

He sunk his head into his hands. "Two. My grand-children."

Laura read the bold hand: *To whom it may concern among the Holborn Guardians.*

"What's it about?" said Amy. "Do you know?"

"I've a notion."

"Your kiddies not in any trouble I hope."

He raised his head and looked at them both directly for the first time, so that Laura felt taken aback as if at the sudden appearance of quite another person, for his eyes as they fixed onto hers, had, after all, kept some private quality that still revealed grief and anxiety, even anger. He said harshly to Amy, "What's going on in there?"

"What do you mean?" said Amy.

"Don't you know they're sick in there? Don't you know they're dying?"

Laura went cold inside her. She heard Amy say indignantly, "They're never dying. They couldn't die and no one know. He'd have to have old Mr Armitage to bury them, now wouldn't he? He couldn't just hide them away. And there's been no burying done since Mrs Hodge, third Sunday in Advent, of that I am sure. Here. Who's been telling you tales? Why, young Mr Bolinger was there no time ago, wasn't he, Laura? And he didn't say anything. He'd have had to have done, being all but in the cloth."

"I tell you they're dying all right. He told me so."

"Now who told you? Someone's been telling tales as shouldn't. What did you go for anyway, to see your kiddies?" She broke off, awed. "They're never dead."

"No." He dropped his head into his hands again. "At least I saw the bigger one. I rang the bell at the gate like they say to, and after a while this man comes out to me. I said, 'I've come to see my two grandsons. I've come to take them out for a bit.' 'Well,' he says, 'you can't take them out.' I'd walked and waited half the day by then and I was that worn I could scarcely stand and I says, 'But I've come all the way from Holborn. Last time they let me take them out.' 'Well,' he says, 'it's not possible.' So I says, 'Well bring them here to me where I can speak with them.' So then he goes away and back he comes with the big lad and I says, 'There's two of them I've come to see. What have you done with the little one?' and the big one says, 'He's sick. They took him away to the sick room and they won't let me go to him.' "

"Why wouldn't they let him?" said Laura. She could not free her mind of Will standing at the railings and Jamie shut away from him, ill. But the man merely glanced at her and went on with what he was saying.

"Then I looks at him and I thinks: All's not well here, for he's all doubled-up like, when he's talking, with his arms held across him and I says to him, 'Have you the gripe in your belly, lad?' and he says, 'Yes, something awful,' like he can scarcely speak. Then the man says, 'You see, he couldn't have come with you anyway, so be off with you and don't make trouble.' Then I saw another man come to the door and this man I knows to be Mr Drouet because I'd seen him once before and I calls out, 'Why, someone must look to this boy because he's sick.' And then he frowns and starts to hurry towards me down the path as if to silence me, and he calls out, 'Here, are you from Holborn?' 'Yes,' I says, and he says, 'You take this letter then and give it to the first person you meet in authority at Holborn Union.' 'Very well,' I says, 'but first you tell me what my boy's sick with, and why no one looks to this big boy who's sick too.' And he shrugs and scowls and says, 'There's

195

lots of them ill.' Then he says, 'It's not my fault they fall ill. I'm not to know what's causing it. They're dying in there very fast at the rate of three or four a day.' Just like that he said it. Then he gives me the letter through the bars and turns on his heel, and each of them takes my boy by an arm and they walk him away from me and he turns his head over his shoulder to me but he never says another word."

"What's his name?" said Laura. Both the man and Amy were staring at her but she could not help herself. "What's his name?"

"What's whose name?" said Amy sharply.

"The big boy who was ill who had the little brother he couldn't get to."

"He's not what you'd call big," said the old man sadly. "He was six before Christmas." But had he meant the big one or the little one? She could not be sure.

"What's his name?" she insisted. Strangely, tears were running down her cheeks. A bell jangled over the kitchen door. Barty was saying something. She heard Amy run out of the room. The old man's face was very close to hers and now it seemed to Laura that he looked at her as if he hated her. "What's it to you, miss?"

"They're my friends," she said. "Jamie, Will. I don't know their other name."

"Friends," he said bitterly. "And what might you mean by friends? Anyway, my kids aren't called that. The eldest's Michael and the little lad's called John. Are they your friends too, miss?"

How could he speak so unkindly to her? It made her stop crying but she seemed to ache all over. "No," she said. "No. But had I known them, they would have been. I tried to feed them, believe me I did."

She heard Amy come hastily up behind her. "What have you been saying to her to make her cry?" She put her arm round Laura's shoulders, but the embrace Laura had wanted for days lay heavily on her like a yoke. "There, there," Amy was saying. "Dry your eyes now and go in looking like nothing's happened or we'll have her out here." Then she turned on the pauper. "That's no way to repay a piece of Christian kindness, to go upsetting her! She's a good girl and a lady and she's never done an ounce of wrong in her life and if she has, she did it for someone else. That I'll swear."

But it came too late. Laura washed her face in the scullery and smoothed her hair and went towards the sitting room without looking at either of them. The old man she never saw again.

CHAPTER EIGHTEEN

When Laura came quietly into the room and took her seat by the window without a word, only Miss Roylance noticed that she was very pale and looked as if she had been crying. Could she be ill? Rather, she seemed to labour under some great anxiety. She would have liked to call Laura over to sit beside her, but in this unwelcoming room she dared not. She wished that she had prevailed on Miss Armitage to stay at home, for really it was too cold for her. But Miss Armitage had insisted upon coming, and now already, rosy and weary from her walk, she was nodding in her chair and would soon be fast asleep.

The table had been pulled over to the fire and the ladies sat around it. Henry downcast and awkward sat a little way from them. Miss Lawton had placed a pair of very small spectacles on her nose and taken from her reticule a folded letter. She opened it, held it up before the spectacles and then at the last offered it suddenly to Aunt Bolinger. "But won't you, my dear? Would it not be more fitting in your own house?"

Aunt Bolinger said, a little grimly, "She did not send the letter to me."

"Oh, very well, dear. As you know, Mrs Rees-Goring is not amongst us, being away since Christmas visiting with her sister." She paused respectfully at the mention of that lady. "But she was gracious enough to write to me — to us all — and suggest that as the needier children have what warm clothes they require for the winter, we turn our attention to holland aprons to be worn in the classroom. Here are her very words: *These would preserve what clothes they have and hide any little unsuitabilities that might occur during the summer months, giving a uniform appearance.*" Miss Lawton beamed about her. She could not have put it nearly so well herself. "Are we all agreed? Shall I put in an order for the holland?"

"It's all one to me," said Aunt Bolinger. She was watching the schoolmistress. "But of course I cannot speak for everyone present."

Miss Roylance said quietly, "You know my views, Miss Lawton."

"But those were views you held at our last meeting. Surely you have changed them."

"No," said Miss Roylance, "I seldom change. I believe our time would be better spent sewing flannel petticoats for the children next door. Why, on Christmas Eve afternoon," she turned impulsively towards Henry, "I saw one of those children through the railings — did we not Mr Bolinger? — attempting to skip in so thin and worn a garment I'm sure she must have felt the cold most cruelly."

199

He sat staring wretchedly at her, hearing his mother say, "If she were cold then she should have stopped skipping and gone inside."

Miss Roylance said, "I know that I am alone in this and shall of course sew whatever you like."

Miss Armitage roused herself then and patting her hand, said, "Of course you are not alone, Margaret. There are some friends in this room. I am sure I saw Henry as I came in, and is not that sad child Laura? And surely Barty is somewhere in the room."

Barty lay on his stomach behind the black armchair in which his aunt was seated. She had commanded him to be present, but to make no sound and to be seen as little as possible. Accordingly he lay out of sight. The women's conversation washed to and fro like a distant sea. He reached under the chair and drew out between the woven strands of canvas a long black horsehair. He began to wind it tightly and neatly around and around the end of his finger. First the flesh went white and then it went purple. He watched it with interest. It did not hurt but it began to beat. He thought perhaps he had better take it off. He unwound it again and watched the colour drain away. Boredom ached in his arms and legs. He rolled quietly onto his back but he was no more comfortable. When he heard Miss Armitage say his name he got up and went and stood behind Miss Roylance's chair, leaning his arm along the back of it and resting his chin on the cuff of his jacket. Miss Roylance sat stiffly forward taking no support from the chair. Between the neck of her dress and the knot of hair from which soft wisps escaped, her skin was very red. She was saying to his aunt, "But I have already written to Mrs Drouet. Naturally at the same time I sent a letter to Mrs Rees-Goring telling her what I had done and offering to resign if she wished it."

Are they arguing? Barty wondered. What do they find to argue about?

Aunt Bolinger looked with a hard triumph over to her son. "You must be tired with this talk, Henry. I'm sure I am."

Will they send her away? thought Laura. Will she go to the asylum? Will she find anything if she goes? But the questions no longer seemed to lead anywhere. She let her sewing lie in her lap and stared out onto the green where two village boys waged a silent remote war against one another, running, mouthing, hurling clods of earth against an uneasy grey sky. Horse's hooves sounded in the road. A single horseman rode with frantic haste past the house. She no longer imagined he had come for her. She watched him rein and turn and enter the side gate that led to Drouet's yard without curiosity, for it could not concern her.

The smell of the glass and the cold leading tingled in her throat. Even as she stared the sky began to creep and hurl at her little wavering flecks of grey. The snow seemed to fly horizontally, splaying out as it reached the window. She stared and stared out at its endlessly renewed, silent, powerless onslaught on the window, on her.

She heard the rattle of crockery and saw that Amy had brought in the tea things and stood now to one side whispering to her aunt. They turned once and looked at her with their lips moving silently. Miss Lawton was saying eagerly by the table, "I do not know if I should mention it, but I have heard the most extraordinary rumours in the village; that Mr Drouet does not have half the children there that he says he does, for he admits them and does away with them, hides them under the floor-boards and continues to charge the workhouse for feeding them. For who's to know in all that mass of children whether they are there or not?"

"Oh no," cried Miss Roylance. "There can be no truth in that." She held out her little hands in front of Barty as if to ward off from him such evil fancies.

"It is true," said Laura suddenly. "At least in a way it's true, some of it. The man said . . ."

Her aunt passing Laura on her way back to the table said in a low voice, "And what would you know about the truth, miss?"

She knows, thought Laura. But she felt nothing.

Barty at that moment saw the grey crawling surface of the window and a second later recognised it for what it was. "Snow!" he cried. "Snow!"

"Barty," said his aunt indignantly, but he ignored her. He caught Miss Roylance's hands and began dragging her onto her feet and over to the window, while she laughed and caught at her gloves and her handkerchief as she rose and went with him. Laura started to follow, but her aunt said, "Laura, stay where you are," and she sat down again.

"Oh, that is exciting," Miss Roylance was saying to Barty, but with a little turn of the head, hoping that Henry might share her pleasure, but seeing no excitement in his face, she was immediately aware that she had spoken foolishly and moved too rapidly about the room, and went back to her chair.

"May I go outside?" said Barty.

"No," said his aunt.

Barty took up his stance behind Miss Roylance's chair. While his aunt poured tea he whispered into her ear, "Will it be deep?"

"It might be."

"Do you want to hear a riddle?"

"Oh yes."

He slid his arm around her neck and whispered so close that she had to draw away a little, "Little white flowers come out of the sky. When the sun comes out they're wet not dry. Little white petals all over the ground. When the sun comes out they're not to be found."

"Why, that's very good," she said kindly. "But I know the answer. I'm sure I do." She laid her hands lightly on his shoulders and whispered against his ear, "Snow, is it not?" Barty beamed and nodded. "Now go and whisper it to Miss Armitage, very gently, because I think she may be asleep."

He ran to Miss Armitage. He could feel his aunt's eyes hard upon him but the snow and Miss Roylance's approval had elated him. Miss Armitage woke with a little jerk of her head when he came up to her, but she was not at all startled and smiled at him benignly. "What is it, Barty?"

He pressed his face to hers so that the stiff lace on her cap brushed his cheek and he smelt the musty stifled smell of summer lavender from her clothes. He repeated the riddle.

"Why," she said gripping his hands and holding him away so that she could see his expectant face, "that is an excellent riddle. One of the best I have heard. I have no idea what the answer can be. Have you, Margaret?"

"Oh, I guessed," said Miss Roylance.

"Won't you tell it to me?" said Miss Lawton.

Barty went and whispered to her scarcely less willingly. Light seemed to fall upon him. He was happy for the first time in days.

His aunt's voice said, "Barty, come to me and I shall tell you a riddle." He stopped where he was with his hands gripping the arm of Miss Lawton's chair and turned to stare at her, mistrusting the look of excitement and pleasure that moved just beneath the stern surface of her face. Everyone was silent, watching not Barty now but the aunt. Laura felt a chill movement in her stomach.

"Well?" said Aunt Bolinger. "Aren't you going to come?"

He went slowly towards her unable to free himself of her eyes. "Come now," she said. She laid her heavy arm on his shoulders but spoke outwards into the room looking from one to the other and half-whispering loud enough for them all to hear. "Go and ask your sister Laura who took what out of the larder on Christmas Day and where she put it."

Her dark eyes bore in on him. He knew that he was being triumphed over by her but he could only say, whispering himself, "I don't know the answer."

"I don't want your answer," said his aunt. "I want hers." She turned him around by the shoulders so that he was facing Laura. He saw Laura's pale wretched face. Then her hands flew up to cover it. She burst into tears and ran from the room.

Henry was on his feet saying in distress, "Mother, why upset her so?"

"I will not tolerate thieving in my house. She has accused herself. She deserves to be shamed, and punished."

Henry said angrily, "She is no thief."

"You saw how she behaved. Amy and I had reason to believe she took it. Now I am certain."

"I'm sure," said Miss Roylance, "that she had no evil purpose."

"Surely you do not count stealing as good, ever?"

It was what she herself had said when Laura had appealed to her. She said softly to Miss Armitage, "We had better be going now before the snow settles."

"I do not understand," said Miss Armitage. "Why was that child made to cry like that?" She sat upright in the chair with her hands clasped in her lap, looking as if she might cry too.

"There," said Miss Roylance. "I'm sure there has been a misunderstanding, but we cannot help by staying. Come now, we must wrap you warmly against the snow. You will enjoy walking in it, will you not?"

"Yes," she said rising. "I shall be glad to walk home." She went slowly towards Aunt Bolinger with her hand loosely extended as if to say goodbye, but instead she said, "I have always hated to see a child made to cry," and walked past her into the hall.

Unwillingly Henry caught his mother's raised eyes, her look of scorn. He called past her, "I'll come with you. I'll see you home."

His mother said, "Barty can go with them since they're so partial to him. Miss Lawton is alone. You are to go with her when she is ready to leave. I shall make your excuses."

He turned bitterly back into the room and stood by the window at the far end while they prepared to leave in the hall. Already a thin mean film of snow clung to the blackened branches of the apple trees and the top of Drouet's wall. He thought: I'll go and call on them tomorrow and apologise. I shall take Laura with me and that will reassure them. He wondered where Laura might have gone. If Miss Lawton stayed as she often did to discuss the departed guests there might be time to find the child and learn the truth and effect some kind of reconciliation. For it was inconceivable that Laura was a thief. Yesterday evening she had sat at the table so troubled and he had scarcely listened to her, his mind full of other things, but she had said nothing about the pie. He was sure of that.

He heard the front door close and crossing the room quickly he watched disconsolately through the front windows the tall cloaked figure of Miss Armitage and the small figures of Margaret and Barty all stooping and moving slowly through the snow. He felt that he had behaved shabbily but scarcely knew how. He began to pace the length of the room hearing the intent mutter of conversation between Miss Lawton and his mother in the hall.

It was then that he heard repeated screaming from behind the house. In the seconds when the screams remained formless, his mind fought against them. Children, he thought. Children playing. But the sound did not relent. It caught in his brain. For the voice was screaming his own name. In terror. *"Cousin Henry! Cousin Henry!"*

He ran through the door down the passage. His mother's face, Miss Lawton's, Amy's in the kitchen, turned past him in amazement. He shouted, "Laura, where are you?" The snow flicked in his mouth and his eyes. He ran towards her stumbling figure coming up through the orchard.

She was not aware that she was screaming. The sound of her voice following her through the trees seemed to be the thing she fled from. She had gone for refuge to the barn and there just inside the doors had found Lizzie.

Laura never regained any recollection of seeing her there. She could never believe that she had touched her, lifted aside her hair, even stooped to look closely at her. But running up between the snatching trees, pursued by fear and the terrible sound that seemed quite disassociated from herself, she knew with certainty that Lizzie was dead.

CHAPTER NINETEEN

In the yard Henry met Laura and caught her by the shoulders. It seemed that he was shouting too. She stopped screaming and stood staring at him working her lips in and out as if trying to form words that would not come.

He heard his mother's voice call, "Who is it? What's the matter?" and heavy footsteps running down the passage by the house. A lantern was coming towards him and voices. Then they stood beside him, the cowman and the ostler from the Castle, grave, concerned, saying one after the other, "What's happened?"

"She's been in the barn," said the cowman. "They go down there. I've often seen them."

Amy came running from the house with a shawl. She gripped Laura in a hard angry embrace, whispering in her ear, "There there, what frightened you then?"

But there were no words to tell. She thought if they would be quiet she might explain. There was no hurry. Nothing to be done. If they would be quiet and listen, but they continued to speak and to hold on to her when she wanted to go inside. Their faces were all about her but it seemed that they pressed and shouted against glass. She saw the distorted faces, the dark urgent mouths, but could neither make them hear, nor grasp what they were saying to her.

"Was it that old man, Laura?"

"What man?" Henry's voice.

"He was here and frightened her this afternoon. I didn't hear what he said but she was crying."

"In the barn, you think?"

"Someone from around here?"

"No."

"You take her inside. We'll see to him."

How confused and mistaken they were. In the kitchen they sat her in Uncle Bolinger's chair. Amy knelt on the floor saying in a whisper, "What did he do, Laura? What did he do?" She was aware of Aunt Bolinger and Miss Lawton standing at the kitchen door staring at her but not saying a word. She leant back in the chair and when she had taken a deep breath she said slowly, trying to make them understand, "It wasn't him. It was Lizzie. She's dead."

But they did not understand. They did not know who Lizzie was. They did not believe that anyone lay like that on the floor of the barn. She said, "I want Papa." Then she lay back in the chair. She was aware how still her hands lay in her lap. She felt very quiet. There was no hurry. Nothing to be done. She would wait like this until Papa came and then she would explain to him.

*

209

Henry stood over the body in the straw saying in his head, or aloud, he did not know, *Oh my God! My God!* He thought: What am I meant to do?

The cowman knelt beside the child holding the lantern. He had turned her over and closed her eyes, decently, respectfully. A man like that, thought Henry, knows exactly what to do and I do not. No one has told me.

"You'd better take her up to the house, sir."

"Yes," he said. "Yes, of course."

"Shall I carry her, sir?"

"No," said Henry. "I'll take her." He thought: This is the first act of my ministry. If I fail in this I fail in all of it. He made an awkward movement, having no idea how to lift or hold her.

The cowman said, "Don't you touch her yet. I'll wrap her in a sack. She's all soaked through, poor mite."

He had seen and smelt it, but he said in surprise, "Is that why she's dead?"

"I shouldn't wonder, sir."

He stood not watching, holding out his arms stiffly until the slight burden was laid across them. Then he began to walk towards the lighted windows of the house, thinking: What do I do now?

Behind him he heard the men's boots and their strong awed voices. "How long d'you think she'd been there?"

"She must have taken sick and crawled in there to die, poor soul."

"Do you think she might be from Drouet's place, sir?"

"Yes," Henry said. He seemed to know without

doubt. He walked more quickly. He could not possibly have confronted his mother with this. Now he knew where to go. He walked past the kitchen door aware that people stood there, but not looking to see who. No one spoke. He went out into the road. There were people there, too, standing in a black group in the thin pools of light thrown onto the snow by the lights of the Castle. It seemed that as he walked footsteps fell in behind him, but at Drouet's gate only he and the cowman continued up the trampled snow on the path, up the wet steps. The cowman reached past Henry and rang the bell. The door was opened by a girl who saw the body and ran away, shouting indistinctly to someone inside.

They followed her through the door. The girl had taken her candle with her so that the hall was almost entirely dark. A door left open to a lamplit room just showed the curving banisters of a handsome old stairway. Somewhere in the distance they heard the sound of shouting and running footsteps. A moment later the faint aureole of a candle came swaying along the ceiling of the upstairs landing. A man in an apron leant over the banisters, lowering his candle over the rail by the length of his arm, frowning, shouting, "And who the hell are you?"

He began to run downstairs. Henry called to him, "Henry Bolinger. I live next door. I found this," and he held out the burden he wanted this angry man to release him from.

He did not take the child but took her chin in the fingers of one hand and turned her wasted face to and fro in the candlelight as expertly and delicately as if she were alive. Thank God, thought Henry. He knows what he is doing. He is not afraid. He found that he himself was trembling. When the man, a gentleman — you could tell — a doctor it seemed, said, "Where did you find this one?" he began to stammer.

The cowman said quietly, "He's very shocked, sir, not being used to it. She was in his barn, sir. No one knew she was there. One of the children staying in the house found her."

The doctor said to Henry, "So you live next door. How much do you know?"

"Nothing."

"Nothing? Not a word in the village of what's going on here?"

"Not a word."

"And the rest of the village?" He turned to the cowman. "How much contact is there with this place?"

"None at all that I know of, sir."

And Henry echoed, "None at all. None at all."

The man stared at him a moment. "Good God, then you'd better see what you've been harbouring. Not you," he said to the cowman. "You stay where you are." He said to Henry, motioning him up the stairs, "You seem to be a gentleman." Their footsteps rang on the marble stairs. "I'll need someone to spread a reasonable account of the truth." The voice behind Henry seemed to drive him on. The candlelight rocked his shadow on the walls. A woman flattened herself against the passage wall hiding a child's face against her apron as he passed. The doctor reached around him to open a door, saying, "In there, over to your left. Find a space for her if you can." The stench of sickness, solid and vicious, was pressed against his face.

At last he was truly come among Drouet's children. In a low, cold, ill-lit room, the floor slippery with filth, they lay all around him, dead and dying lying three in a bed, some quite still, some screaming and moaning in pain. He stood while they lifted the dead child out of his arms and looked about him, knowing what he saw to be real, but feeling his own existence to be quite unreal. He heard his own voice repeating, "What is it? In God's name, what is it?"

"Why, don't you know?" said the doctor's voice. "It is the cholera."

Laura still sat without moving by the kitchen fire. Barty crouched on a stool beside her with his head on her knee, hating her silence. Amy moved automatically about the kitchen clearing away a meal that no one had eaten.

They heard Henry let himself in by the side door. They heard the violent creaking of the scullery pump, the water splashing, the sound of retching. When he opened the door and came into the kitchen, he was deathly pale. His eyes, they saw, were full of tears.

"Oh dear God, what is it?" said Amy.

"It's cholera," he said. "In Drouet's place." He looked at the children. "They must be got away from here at once."

Amy said, "Your ma will go half out of her mind when she hears. I'll tell her, though. Don't you go near her looking like that."

Laura wondered how long it would be before they might go. She stared at her cousin, feeling nothing for him, no pity or concern. He held a lighted candle in his hand and she noticed that the flame was reflected again and again in the tears in his eyes as if single candles had been set in a long vista of empty rooms.

Later Amy shook her and said, "You're not to sit like that any more. You're to come with me." She brought Laura her cloak and wrapped her shawl around her head and gripping one of her hands and one of Barty's she set out with them through the village. They were going to the church. A group of village women waited in the snow opposite the carriage gate of the church as Drouet's children had on Christmas Day. They stood with them, hearing the word *cholera* pass and repass them like a strange whisper. "It's the way he runs that place," said Amy. "It's brought the cholera on us."

They heard the grinding of wheels and saw, the way they had come, lanterns and torches in the dark street. The undertaker's carts drew up, leaving long wavering black trails behind them in the snow. Six large coffins were scraped off the back of the carts and jolted on to the bearers' shoulders.

Amy whispered, "Those are never children's coffins! That or he's got more than one in there."

They trooped into the graveyard to the side of a great hole dug behind the church. Old Mr Armitage was waiting for them with a grey knitted shawl wrapped over his black gown. Miss Roylance stood beside him, holding his arm. He stood in the biting snow with his

214

white hair blowing from under the rim of his tall black hat, fumbling in the prayer book with his mittened fingers. *Forasmuch as it has pleased Almighty God of His great mercy to take unto Himself the souls of our dear children here departed ... name ... name ... Lizzie Brown...* That was Lizzie. She was truly dead then. Dead and buried. I was not kind to her, Laura thought. The names went on. There were so many. She strained to hear them spoken in the frail voice. *We therefore commit their bodies to the ground; earth to earth, ashes to ashes, dust to dust.* There were no more. No James. No William. They were safe. It was over. The cold hard earth rattled on the coffin lids. Mr Armitage was led away.

Amy was gripping Laura's arm. "Did you hear that?" she was saying. "What he done? Crammed them six in a coffin!" She began to shout: "Wouldn't even let them lie decent in the earth! Six in a coffin, damn him! Six in a coffin!"

James Andrews sat in the bus. They were taking him away. Will had taken him to see the horse and now he sat on the bus on William McDougall's knee with Will beside him. His head ached and he felt very tired. When they lifted the tarpaulin to let another boy into the van the strange excited light off the snow hurt his eyes. There were people in the streets standing watching them, waving and smiling. He wondered who they were. "Where are we going?" he said to Will.

"Hospital somewhere."

"Is that good, Will?"

215

"Yeh," said Will. "Yeh. You bet. Better than here, isn't it?"

"Yeh. Sure to be. I'm hungry," he said to Will. But he said it more out of habit than conviction. His whole body ached.

A shout. The whip cracked. The cart jolted forward. The boys raised a cheer. The people on the road side cheered and waved and among them, to his surprise, because he had never really wondered where she came from, was the young lady who had brought him food, waving, smiling. He would have sat up and waved back but he felt too tired. He leant back against William McDougall and put his hands to his head to make the pain go away.

"I saw him," Laura said to Barty. "I saw him, and Will was with him." She caught him by the hand and ran with him into the road, waving and shouting although the black tarpaulin cover had fallen back into place and the only faces she knew had vanished. The cold clean air ached in her throat. The people cheered. The black vans rumbled away. She put her arm tightly around Barty's shoulders. "It's all right," she said. "They're safe. They got away."

One of the nurses at the Royal Free Hospital saw him sitting in the clothes he had worn from the asylum on the end of his bed, crying because he must sleep in a bed by himself and Will had been put with some older boys in another room. "There," she said. "There. You've nothing to cry about now."

He cried with his head in his hands as if it were too heavy to support. He's tired out, she thought. He should be in bed. "Are you hungry?" she asked him.

"Yeh," he said.

"Come then." She took him by the hand, stopping to look at it with a kind of pitying disapproval when she felt the broken skin. "We'll have you right soon," she said. She led him to the fire at the end of the ward, and sat him on a little stool. "I'll get you some supper," she said. "Then you can go to bed."

She brought him a mug of warm milk and a piece of bread. He sat up then and took the bread in his hand, feeling it. Then he said quite clearly, "What a big piece of bread," and looked up at her with a wondering expression.

"Here, you drink this," she said. She knelt on the floor beside him and held the cup of milk to his mouth and he sucked at it over the rim until it was all gone. Then he pulled at the soft part of the bread with his teeth, but after a few bites he handed it back to her and shook his head.

She undressed him by the fire, and pulled a clean nightshirt over his head. There's nothing to him, she thought. As she tucked him into the great empty bed she said, "What's your name?"

"Jamie. Jamie Andrews."

When next she passed the bed and looked at him he was asleep. At six in the morning he woke in the first stage of cholera. By eleven-thirty he was dead.

"I don't suppose anyone knows what he was called," said the doctor looking down at him. He had picked up the little shirt on the foot of the bed. No name. No number. Hopeless.

"I know," said the nurse. "He told me. James Andrews."

"Are you sure?" he said, writing it quickly on the back of a bill he had crammed in his pocket. "Would you testify if it came to that?"

She remembered holding the mug for him. "Yes," she said. "I'll do what you like."

"That's good of you." He wrote her name too, Mary Harris. "We've got the time he died. We'll check his name. Can you give a description of the state he was in? Can you remember one from another?"

"Yes," she said. "I remember him."

In the vault of Trinity Church in the Gray's Inn Road, by the light of a single lantern a surgeon dissected the body of James Andrews. His hands were clumsy with cold. The two students who worked with him, the one placing the organs in jars, the other taking dictation, wore their scarves across their faces, but he had let his fall. The smell was tolerable in winter. Besides he wanted his voice to be quite clear. There was to be an inquest, perhaps a trial. His evidence would be called. This was the child they hoped to use. It's all nonsense, he thought. He dictated slowly as he worked. *"Pustular itch on hands and face. Belly distended. Muscles relaxed. Limbs wasted. Flesh soft and flabby. A total absence of fat even on those parts where it is generally thickest."*

"So they're going to have an inquest. They'll never

get the man that ran the place sent for trial," said the student. They had done, and walked through the frozen churchyard with their hands in their pockets.

"They'll have a damn good try."

"What can they charge him with?"

"Manslaughter."

"They haven't a hope."

"No," said the surgeon. "He's safe as houses. He didn't kill the child. It died of cholera. Besides, you saw it. There was nothing to it. A sickly constitution. It would have died anyway most likely. It's all a lot of damned nonsense."

Laura sat in the carrier's cart next to her father. Barty on the other side of him slumped asleep with his cap over his eyes. Laura sat upright with her eyes open, holding very tightly to Papa's hand. He had come that morning, suddenly been standing in the kitchen holding out his arms. For a moment she had not believed it. They had sent for him the night before but they had not told her.

He had not seen Aunt Bolinger who did not leave her room, but he had prayed for a time with Henry and spoken with him, piecing together what he could of his children's part in the tragedy. He wondered if Laura, too, would be distressed, would want to pour out to him what she had seen and heard, but she was very quiet, her face smooth and content, even happy, as they rolled along in the cart.

From time to time he asked anxiously, "How do you feel? Do you feel all right?"

"Yes. Yes. Of course."

He was surprised that she laughed.

Why does he worry? she thought. The leather curtains of the cart were drawn. It was dark and cold, but so safe holding at last to his hand. She thought she had never felt happier.

CHAPTER TWENTY

And the happiness continued. When, in the mornings, Laura's eyes opened to the walls of her own bedroom, she lay in a state of conscious happiness and relief that she had never known before she went away. She watched the tilting rectangles of sunlight cast by the window frame quiver over the blue flowers on the paper until they seemed alive, and felt the same vibration of life and joy inside herself as if each waking were a reprieve from something she dreaded.

But what could that be? She never so far as she knew had bad dreams.

Once she woke in what seemed darkest night and saw her father's face, sharply lit by the candle he held, looking anxiously down at her. Laura sat straight up, filled with fear. "What is the matter? Are you ill?" She could hear that her voice was jerky and high-pitched. She was not fully awake.

"No, no," he said. "Of course not." He laid the candle-stick on the mantelshelf and sat on the edge of the bed. "I was worried about you. I came to reassure myself."

"Did I cry out? Did I have a bad dream?"

"No, no. So long as you are all right—you are not troubled."

It occurred to her then that he might still fear for her health. "But I can't be ill now, can I?"

"No. There's no danger of sickness now."

"It was so very long ago."

"Was it, dearest?" He rested the back of his hand against her cheek which had sunk back on the pillow and smiled, for she had spoken as if it were years not months since she, a sensitive child, his child, whose awareness they had always protected so carefully, had seen that thing whose sight and stench he knew too well. Dear God, he thought, and found that he had involuntarily withdrawn his hand. She will carry that dead child within her all her life.

When he reached out to touch her again he saw that she was asleep, and lowering the candle as he left, could not doubt the perfect contentment on her still face.

He was mistaken if he thought that Laura kept any recollection of Lizzie lying dead. It was Lizzie's living presence that stayed with her. Strangely she felt no curiosity about the two boys, who at the time had concerned her more. If ever she thought of them it was to see again their faces close together in the back of the bus that instant before the black tarpaulin fell. They had moved on. They were safe. But Lizzie, who had no one, stayed with her, and in their imaginary talks had come to look and sound very like Laura herself: a presence like that reflection of her own face on the van window that had appeared out of the cold and the dark and followed so persistently all the way to Tooting. It was scarcely a haunting. For days she would not think of Lizzie at all. Then at some moment when her thoughts were not occupied, Lizzie would be with her. The cold hand would slip into hers, not gripping or tugging but lying there patiently, waiting for the time when Laura would, as she knew she must, venture out again to those regions she had first penetrated in her aunt's barn.

One evening the family had gathered around the drawing room table to share the lamplight. Laura's mother drew from her workbox a folded letter. "This is from your Aunt Bolinger," she said looking quickly from one child to the other. "I thought you might like to hear her news." They neither spoke nor raised their eyes to her. Laura sat sewing, dark hair smooth on smooth brow. Barty might not have heard. His face was peaceful and intent, his hands delicately fitted together his latest treasured gift from the cook, the yellow waxy bones of a pig's trotter, with a pure mechanical pleasure.

Their mother did not reprove their silence, but read aloud from the letter, how no one else in the village had contracted the disease, which was considered by some, less hard-headed than Aunt Bolinger herself, to be little short of a miracle. Drouet's house was empty now and there was talk of raising a public subscription to tear it down. It appeared that the schoolmistress had gone to a new appointment somewhere in the north and that a far more suitable replacement had been found. Cousin Henry wrote cheerfully from Oxford.

Laura continued to sew, aware of her father's eyes upon her. He wished to know what she felt, but it seemed to Laura that she was feeling very little, less perhaps than she should, for the dwindled figures of her aunt and her Cousin Henry. Only at the thought of Miss Roylance sitting alone in a coach, feeling the distance lengthen from that house she had wished never to leave, did her heart wince.

Her mother finished the letter and folded it and put it away. After a moment's silence Laura said, "Will you read to us now, Papa?"

He was reading them the instalments of *David Copperfield* which was perhaps why he chose one evening later in March to read to Laura one of Mr Dickens' passionately angry articles in the *Examiner* on what he called the "paradise" at Tooting. The details of the inquest and of Drouet's trial for manslaughter — some of which were quite distressing — he had of course kept from her, and forbade the servants to mention the matter in the children's hearing. Nevertheless he felt she had a right to know the moral issue—that it was even his duty to take it up with her.

When he had done, he looked across to where she sat on a little stool by the fire in his study. "So you see, Laura, in spite of what Mr Dickens feels, the jury found him innocent."

She said without any question in her voice, "But he was guilty, Papa."

He said gently, "They brought him to trial for causing the death of a single child. They could not prove that any action of his had caused that child to contract cholera."

She looked for a long time into the fire. He wished she would say something. At last he said, "Did you ever see Mr Drouet?"

"Once. Outside the church."

"Did he look a wicked man?"

"No," she said remembering. "But he is guilty of something. God would think him so."

"Yes," he said, "I think he is." She began to cry then, and he stretched out his arms to her saying in distress, "Oh Laura, I should not have mentioned it."

She came to him and leaning her head against his shoulder, said in a voice sadder than he could have imagined, "I did wrong. I did wrong."

"Not to tell what you knew?" For it must be that that troubled her.

She hung her head seeing her shoes, the legs of the table, the hearthrug, the fender, knowing she was not meeting his eyes. "I told lies. I stole the pie."

She heard him sigh and imagined it was the sound of his love withdrawing. It was only bewilderment. She had of course in a way been right to lie and steal. She alone apparently had felt for those wretched children what he would have a child of his feel, but would he in his position be wise to tell her that? Would it fortify her in the next temptation that came to her? She was very dear to him. He put his arm around her and kissed her hair. "Tell me, dearest, why didn't you tell anyone that you knew those children were ill-treated?"

"There was no one to tell," Laura said.

HISTORICAL NOTE

Much of this book is based on fact. In the autumn of 1847 a Mr Bartholomew Drouet wrote to several workhouses in London advertising a school where boys and girls might be instructed in a variety of useful trades that would enable them to earn their way in the world and thus break the cycle of pauperism to which it was feared an upbringing in the workhouse might condemn them. The workhouses were crowded, at the time, with children for whom special provision was impossible, and Drouet's offer of *various trades ... taught by well-conducted masters on a large scale so that we are enabled to fit the boys for all kinds of servitude,* and instruction for girls in *needlework, laundry, washing and general housework* was welcome indeed, even at what seemed the exorbitant cost to the parishes of 4s. 6d. per child per week.

Drouet's school was inspected by officials from the interested workhouses who found everything satisfactory. The diet of the children was carefully planned. Tooting was noted for its healthy atmosphere. The high

226

cost of sending the children there was thought in itself to be a guarantee of their good treatment.

The children soon began to arrive in numbers. By the following winter Drouet had exceeded his original limit of 1,200 children by a further 200 and was obliged to throw up new buildings to house them. Adverse reports of the quality of these buildings, the quality of the food and the treatment of the children had begun to reach the workhouse Governors, but Drouet's violent outbursts when criticised and, no doubt, the appalling prospect of re-absorbing all these children made them hesitate to act.

It was a fatal hesitation. In January of 1849 an inspector of the Board of Health confirmed that cholera had broken out in the asylum and 180 children subsequently died. At the main inquest on these children, evidence from the inspecting doctor, relatives, and the surviving children themselves painted a damning picture of overcrowding, poor ventilation, inadequate clothing, primitive sanitation, food that may have been sufficient in quantity but was often of such poor quality as to be inedible, harsh work and harsh discipline. The coroner committed Drouet to trial for the manslaughter of one of the dead children, a six-year-old boy called James Andrews.

The trial took place in April. At that time no one knew the cause of cholera; it was another twenty years before it was discovered that the disease came from germs living in contaminated water. It is clear to us now that the conditions in Drouet's asylum produced the outbreak, and that the weakened health of children kept

227

in such circumstances would have left them with little resistance against disease, but in 1849 no one could be sure that the cholera was not an inexplicable "act of God" quite unconnected with the way the asylum was run. At the trial the judge strongly advised the jury that no one had proved that James Andrews, a sickly child, would ever have been robust enough to endure the terrible disease even if he had never suffered the hardships of his life at Tooting. When the jury found Drouet innocent there was an outburst of applause in the court.

Not everyone agreed. Dickens wrote a series of impassioned articles about the affair, and though the case against Drouet failed in law, the details that emerged of his callous neglect of the large number of children in his care caused a public outcry from certain sections of the community for stricter supervision of similar establishments in the future.

All the parts of this story that deal directly with the asylum are taken from the reports and newspaper accounts of the trial and inquest. The rest — the characters and the lives of the villagers of Tooting — are all imaginary. What happened to Mr Drouet afterwards is not known; he disappears from history.